ONLY ONE COFFIN

A PARANORMAL ROMCOM

A.J. TRUMAN

TRUMAN BOOKS

Copyright © 2022 by A.J. Truman

All rights reserved.

No part of this book may be reproduced in any form or by any electronic or mechanical means, including information storage and retrieval systems, without written permission from the author, except for the use of brief quotations in a book review.

❦ Created with Vellum

ONLY ONE COFFIN

I'm stuck sharing a coffin with the world's perkiest vampire. This vacation is going to suck.

After centuries of eternal existence, and still mourning the loss of my lover to vicious slayers, I needed a few days of peaceful solitude at the Hotel Draugr.

But thanks to a double-booking mishap, I'm forced to share my coffin with Kilroy, a freshly bitten vampire who loves his new afterlife as much as he loves hanging ten. My unexpected roommate is determined to show me how "totally awesome" being a vampire can be.

Doesn't he know vampires don't do sunshine of any kind?

Through epic snowball fights and midnight meetups at vampire speakeasies, the ice around my not-technically-beating heart begins to melt. And during days sharing our too-small coffin, one part of me has trouble staying dead.

Maybe this budding relationship has teeth...that is, if we can evade the slayers closing in on the hotel.

Only One Coffin is a grumpy/sunshine, forced proximity, paranormal MM romcom featuring a 300-year age gap, coffin cuddling, and a vampire bro who wears flip flops no matter how cold it is outside.

To get access to free stories, plus sneak peeks on my new books, join my newsletter.

https://www.ajtruman.com/outsiders/

1

MAGNUS

Each year, I celebrated Christmas the way it was meant to be celebrated: I shut all the curtains, put cotton in my ears to drown out carolers, poured myself a blood martini with three olives, nestled into my coffin, and read books by candlelight until I fell asleep with a page stuck to my cheek.

Happy Holidays indeed.

I was never into the Christmas season, and this was likely the case when I was human, too. The pageantry. The songs. The sticky residue from half-eaten candy canes.

Christmas was all about...joy. And togetherness. And crucifixes.

I would rather drink water.

Vampires weren't about living lives of joy. For one, we weren't living. But more importantly, we lived in the shadows, in the empty spaces of human existence. The world continued turning, but we weren't allowed to be part of it. We settled on the fringes lest we be chased by mobs with stakes and garlic. Did you know how smelly garlic was? It was like being chased by a giant swarm of armpits.

The truth was, I wanted no part of the human world. Humans had futures to look forward to. They had hopes and dreams and plucky attitudes; vampires only had an interminable forever.

Maybe if you were lucky, you had a lover to fritter away the unending days with, a partner in the foxhole of forever, someone with whom you could poke fun at humans (one scroll through social media could give us fodder for days), someone who found purpose in trying to elicit a smile from you.

But not all of us were so lucky.

Or even worse, some of us were lucky once upon a time, and then that luck was cruelly ripped from us.

There was one post-holiday tradition I kept. Every year, on the night after Christmas, I turned myself into a bat and zipped across the Atlantic to stay at The Draugr Hotel in Iceland for a week. It was isolated in a desolate mountain range, surrounded by active volcanoes, and like all vampire vacation spots, unreachable by humans. It was the perfect place to get away from civilization for a few days and relax. Best of all, there were only four dreaded hours of daylight to deal with each day.

I'd been visiting the hotel for a century; unfortunately, they didn't offer a rewards program.

When I arrived in Iceland on that wonderfully frigid December evening, I was greeted by the Northern Lights glinting against the glaciers in the distance. After one hundred years, the sight still did not get old.

Unlike human hotels, there was no grand front entrance. We didn't want to attract attention. A small wooden sign carved with an intricate design and WELCOME in the center hung above the entrance to an unassuming cave. After the usual stroll through cold darkness, the glow of the hotel burned in the distance, a light at the end of this tunnel.

The cave opened up to an enormous, gothic lobby with high ceilings, eroded rock for walls, and a cozy fireplace in the middle. Guests were sprinkled across overstuffed couches and comfy leather armchairs marked with stretches and patches. For some, this was the only time they got to see each other. I never found my way into one of those vampire cliques.

I inhaled the familiar musty scent of the Draugr as if it were the hug of a family member. The outdated carpet and overall dreary aesthetic gave me twinges of nostalgia.

Though to be fair, once I turned 200, everything began making me nostalgic.

The hotel had been around for centuries as a getaway for vampires looking to escape the hustle and bustle of the living world. Vampires from around the world met up here, one of the only places on the planet where we could be our true selves without judgment, out from under the watchful, stake-thirsty eyes of humans.

I strolled up to the front desk located off to the side. The station was tiny compared to the cavernous space and had a neat arrangement of cubby holes behind it. A sign on the desk read MANAGEMENT ASKS THAT YOU NOT BITE THE INNKEEPER.

A wrinkled old human with a bushy mustache turned around; his eyes twinkled with recognition. Humans were always excited about things. It could be highly annoying.

"Magnus! Happy holidays!"

"Happy Holidays, Einar," I said back and meant it. Einar was the only person who got a sincere holiday wish from me. It felt like only yesterday that he was the rambunctious three-year-old running through guests' legs with toy trains in his hand. "How are Petra and the kids?"

"They're not kids anymore. They're in their sixties." He chuckled. This happened a lot for Einar as vampires weren't the best with time. "But they're still kids to me."

"Me, too."

"My grandson Reynar and his wife are expecting this spring. It'll be my third great-grandchild!"

"How wonderful." Einar had a large family, which he showed off in a framed picture on the wall. It was common knowledge that the rules about not biting the innkeeper extended to the innkeeper's family.

Reynar was learning the ropes of the hotel from his grandfather. Einar pointed to him across the lobby screwing another candle sconce into the wall.

"It all goes by so fast. He's going to take over one of these days." Einar beamed at his grandson, who looked just like Einar did fifty years ago.

My eyes flicked back to the framed photo bursting with progeny, and a twinge of envy tightened in my spine.

"Hopefully not for a long time," I said. I knocked on the desk to bring us back to the task at hand. "I come bearing gifts."

I pulled some small wrapped presents from my suitcase. I'd sprung for the special vampire luggage that shrunk when flying. This way, I didn't have to deal with shipping through VPS (Vampire Postal Service) and their high propensity for losing luggage.

"Magnus, you didn't have to do this!"

To reiterate, I was not a holiday person at all. Not in the least. But I did believe in giving people who treated me well small tokens of appreciation. And I wrapped said tokens so it'd be a surprise to him. And the only time I saw Einar was in December. But these were not Christmas gifts.

"I'll put them under my tree," he said.

"They're not Christmas gifts." I didn't have the energy to go down this path of technicalities. "Do with them what you want. Enjoy. It's my pleasure."

"Thank you." Einar put them under the desk. He then rifled through his files to find my reservation, just as he'd done for years and years. But there was a new addition to his station this year.

A computer sat at the end of the desk. He paid it no attention.

"You're finally entering the twenty-first century?" I asked.

"That's all Reynar. He wants to *modernize our infrastructure*," he said with an eye roll. "I told him it's the wrong crowd."

Vampires enjoyed some modern comforts, but for the most part, we eschewed technology. We were hundreds of years old; it was easy to be stuck in our ways.

"He can fiddle with his computer all he wants. I'll stick to paper." Einar pulled out my reservation card and had me sign. He turned to his wall of cubby holes and reached for the key in the lower right corner.

He turned the key in his hand and studied it. "Look, if you ever want to stay in the Hengill Suite again, just say the word. You two always loved that room. Gunnar loved the view."

I held up my hand firmly, keeping a grin on my face for dear dead life. I had only begun my vacation. I should at least unpack before I spiral into a crushing depression. "That's okay. I like this room."

I preferred my current room, tucked away in the corner,

away from the lively chatter, with a view of a severe, bottomless pit.

"There's a lot of new guests this year. Fresh blood, if you will. Everyone is very friendly."

"I just want to relax in my coffin, maybe get a massage, watch the snow fall, work on my pale complexion."

"Okay." Einar gave my hand a small pat as he handed off the key. "I miss him, too," he whispered out.

I had nothing eloquent to say back, so I gave him one final nod and left for my room. I looked forward to not emerging until the new year.

———

SINCE THE HOTEL was built inside a mountain, the hallways of the Draugr were thin and windy. At certain points, the ceiling dipped down. I pitied any blood-drunk vampires trying to make their way back to their room before sunrise. Pictures of local artists from as far back as the Viking era lined the walls. There were lots of pictures to admire since my room was at the end of the hall. After Gunnar perished, I asked Einar for the most secluded room he had.

Some of the doors still used keys, while others were updated to card readers. I was stuck with a card, which wasn't terrible, but I preferred the finiteness of a key. There was only one key, and it was mine.

I heaved out a tired sigh when I reached the door. Another annual trip to Iceland. Another year down. Infinity more to go.

The room was to my liking: dark and cold. The extra-thick curtains were drawn to block out any emerging sunlight. In the darkness, I could make out a rolltop desk in the corner, wardrobe closet, and bathroom entrance. The center of the room was taken up by a large, mahogany coffin sitting on a raised platform. The craftsmanship on these coffins was unlike anything in the human world. Thick, dark wood was etched with custom detailing, the insides lined with silken padding. Even with our superhuman strength, it must've taken four vampires to carry it up the stairs.

Just seeing it made me yawn. I was worn out from traveling; my body craved slumber.

I stripped off my jacket and pants. I unbuttoned my crisp white shirt and hung up all three items in the closet. I climbed the wooden step built into the side and opened the coffin. I'd slept in enough coffins in my after-lifetime to make my way through in the darkness.

I let out a small moan when my feet hit the soft padding. I would sleep very well.

Perhaps I'd gained weight over the past year. I'd had a few blood binges here and there; who didn't let themselves go every now and again? That could explain why the coffin felt tighter than usual.

When I stretched my arms, I felt a mass beside me. Too squishy to be the coffin wall. My first thought was that Einar had put in body pillows. Soft, warm body pillows. I rolled over and pulled it against me.

Did body pillows snore?

"Uhh, dude."

And did they talk?

I lit the small lantern nestled on a shelf against the coffin wall. Two blinking blue eyes stared back at me.

The body pillow screamed.

Just because I was a vampire didn't mean I was immune to being scared.

So I screamed, too.

2

MAGNUS

I jumped up and smacked my head on the coffin lid. Damn mahogany.

"Who are you?" I asked.

"Hey, what's up? The name's Kilroy." His bright, crystal blue eyes remained blown open in surprise.

"Who?"

"Kilroy," he said as if we were meeting at a networking mixer, and not in my coffin where I was supposed to sleep.

His boyish quality and floppy blond hair meant he had to have been bitten when he was no older than twenty-five. And his toned arms and chest meant he'd been a very athletic twenty-five-year-old.

"What's your name?" He held out his hand for a shake, which I didn't reciprocate. "Sorry for screaming earlier. I've never had a stranger climb into bed with me. This is my first time staying at the Draugr. I guess they didn't want to spoil the surprise."

"You're the one surprising me. This is my room." I climbed out of the coffin.

"You're the first vampire I've met who sleeps naked." He

eyed my hairy, almost-naked body. I was wearing underwear, and thank goodness for that.

Where he was lean and smooth, I had a little bit of a gut and middle-aged heft.

Why was I studying this intruder's body?

I pulled my wool jacket from the chair and put it on. "What are you doing in my room?"

"This is my room?"

"Was that a question?"

"Uh, no." He cleared his throat. "Sorry. You're very serious. It's kinda scary."

"Sneaking into someone's room and sleeping in their coffin is very serious. You're not some blood-sucking Goldilocks."

"You could be one of the bears." Kilroy had the nerve to notch a smile.

A smile!

I looked down at my jacket, which was doing a lousy job at covering me. I pulled it closed.

"This isn't funny! How are you laughing right now? Do you like when strangers climb into bed with you?"

He seesawed his head, giving me a litany of questions about his sexual escapades.

"I'm up for anything. I mean, what's the worst someone could do? I'm dead." He shrugged his shoulders.

He ran his fingers along the edge of his puka shell necklace, the white of the shells bringing out his white fangs. He wore a sleeveless T-shirt and sweatpants, which was probably the same outfit he slept in as a human. It seemed like a very human kind of sleep outfit. Vampires either slept fully clothed or naked. There was no in between with us.

"What's your name?"

"Magnus."

"Magnus, I didn't sneak in here. I used my key. I'm booked in this room." From the other side of the coffin, he rustled up his pants from the floor and pulled out a key card. "If I were to sneak into any room, I would choose one with a better view."

I swiped the key card and held it to the faint flame of the Victorian gaslamp on the desk. It matched mine. I took it with me into the hall.

"You're aware you don't have any pants on, right?" I heard Kilroy say through the door.

I waved his card over the sensor. The hum of the door unlocking filled the hall, which fortunately was empty.

I opened the door back into my room and found Kilroy leaning against the coffin like it was a new Corvette, lazy grin slapped on his lips. "Now who's the intruder?"

MINUTES LATER, once I put my pants and shirt on, I tapped incessantly on Einar's concierge bell in the lobby.

Kilroy waited behind me playing with his necklace. He'd thrown on a Hawaiian shirt with a blinding floral design. His feet were crammed into a musty pair of overworn flip-flops. Who brought flip-flops to a mountain in Iceland?

He gazed around at the lobby, bowled over by its scope.

"Is this your first time at the Draugr?" he asked.

"No."

"It's so cool. Like, we're inside an actual-ass mountain." His head went all the way back, I thought it was going to snap off.

"Yes, it's quite a lovely establishment."

"This is the nicest hotel I've ever been in, even counting my human life. I stayed in some real shitholes as a human.

What about you? Where would you rank this hotel on your list?"

"I don't have a list." I tapped the bell again.

"Do you at least have a top five?"

I tapped and tapped and was ready to shake Einar from a sound sleep if I had to.

"Magnus, what can I do for you?" Einar's beaming face froze as soon as he got a look at mine. "Is everything okay?"

"It's not. I found this gentleman in my room."

"Technically, I found you in my room." A gleeful smile escaped Kilroy's lips.

I turned to Einar and rolled my eyes. He wasn't as old as me, but he had to be old enough to find this gentleman annoying.

"Can you help him find his correct room?" I flashed a fake smile at Kilroy. Showing off my fangs would do nothing for him, unfortunately, but hopefully he could pick up on the disdain in my eyes.

He did not. Instead, he gave me a double thumbs up. Vampires were not supposed to be this chipper. We loathed sunshine of all kinds.

"Certainly. One minute." Einar rifled through his papers and pulled up my reservation. "I see here, one room booked for Magnus through January second."

"And just me, correct?"

Einar scanned the paper an extra second, then nodded in the affirmative.

"It's settled." I clapped a hand on Kilroy's shoulder. *Thanks for playing, now scram.* "This is a large hotel. It can be a bit confusing, but Einar can help you find your room. I'll leave your things in a neat pile in the hall."

"Hold up." Kilroy stepped forward with a cocky walk that gave me pause. "Are you sure?"

"Einar is the proprietor of the hotel," I said. "He's sure."

Kilroy pulled a folded-up paper from his pocket, handed it to Einar. "Here's my online confirmation. It says I booked the Vogur Room."

"Online confirmation?" Einar got nervous all of a sudden, like he'd just been asked to solve a calculus equation on the spot.

"Yeah. I booked online."

"Oh." Einar rifled through his papers.

"What do you mean 'oh?'" I asked.

"That's something Reynar set up this year." Einar paged his grandson, who'd been working in the back office.

"Online reservations let you book a room online. Online means the internet, which...hmmm how am I going to explain that one?" Kilroy's face twisted into a befuddled knot.

"You don't need to explain the internet to me. I'm not that old." Actually, I was that old. But I still knew what a bloody computer was. I'd even logged onto the undead dating app Bloodsuckr once, but it wasn't for me.

Reynar shuffled to the front desk. The baby who Einar proudly showed off to guests was now a middle-aged man with a large protruding gut and wavy hair thinning at the top.

"Grandfather, what's wrong?"

"Can you show me how this online reservation system works?" Einar plastered on a friendly smile while Reynar clicked away at the computer, but I could tell he was pissed about this encroachment of technology on his decades-old process. People thought technology made our lives better. But that was true only some of the time. A few inventions were good, e.g. antibiotics and electricity. But the vast majority of technological advancements only seemed to make life more taxing.

"So..." Kilroy let out a chuckle. "We've got ourselves a little conundrum."

"They'll sort it out. They have a combined century of experience running this hotel."

"Totally. They can get you booked into another room. No problem."

"Me?" I asked, holding back an evil glare.

"Well, you haven't unpacked."

"So? It's my room."

"Fair. I can move. I'm just excited to be here. This is my first vampire vacation."

He chuckled again. Kilroy was a fan of chuckling and smiling and acting as if everything was magic and sunbeams. Too bad sunbeams could kill nearly everyone in here.

"We figured out the problem." Einar returned to our end of the front desk. The fact that Reynar stood behind him sheepishly, blush covering his cheeks, did not bode well.

Einar moved aside so his grandson could take center stage.

"The online reservation system has a few kinks we still need to work out," Reynar said. "Reservation confirmations are supposed to be printed off so we can add them to my grandfather's hard copy files. That, unfortunately, did not happen here."

"So you double booked us?" I asked, cutting to the chase.

"I'm very sorry about this," Einar said. "We will refund you for your room."

"That's all right. If you can book Mr. Kilroy into a new room, then everything will be fine." It sounded weird on my tongue to call Kilroy a mister.

"That's cool with me." Kilroy shrugged, just happy to be here it seemed. "Although, since you haven't unpacked, it might be easier for you to move. Just sayin'."

"Gentlemen." Einar held up his hand. "Unfortunately, we are all booked up this week."

"What?" I asked, incredulous.

"I'm very sorry."

"You have absolutely no other rooms?" This was a big mountain. Surely there had to be some abandoned part of the hotel, some extra coffin covered in centuries of dust.

"We have no vacancies. This was a mistake, and I assure you it won't happen again." He turned to Reynar and delivered a very sharp eyebrow raise.

"So what are we supposed to do? There's only one coffin."

"We can share. I'm cool with that," Kilroy said. Of course he was cool. The thought of sharing a coffin with him and his toned body gave me a sudden flash of heat. Wherever *that* came from, I would deal with it later.

"I am *not* cool with it. You're probably a very nice person, Kilroy, but I don't know you, and you don't know me. I think we'd prefer to have our privacy." I adjusted my collar. It was hot in here. The fire was roaring a bit too much. "Surely, there has to be another room available?"

Einar and Reynar shared a look, then shook their heads no in unison.

"We have an air mattress we can inflate," Reynar suggested.

"What about the cots?" Einar asked.

"They were old, so I replaced them with air mattresses. They're all the rage and made from a locally sourced, eco-friendly plastic."

Einar rubbed the spot between his eyebrows. "Our

guests have fangs, Reynar. Sharp, pointy fangs. Those air mattresses won't last through the night."

Grandfather and grandson devolved into a squabble about the direction of the hotel that wasn't bringing us any closer to a solution.

"I have an idea," Kilroy offered, his voice calm in this cloud of chaos. He pointed at the couch near the fireplace. "I can take some of the couch cushions up to the room and sleep on those. It's a comfortable couch."

"You'll have to sleep on the floor," I said.

"I'll be on couch cushions. It's fine. I've camped on the beach and slept on friends' floors. I got this!"

"You still have your memories." A wistful pang plunked into the recesses of my heart.

"Uh, yeah. I'm a vampire, not an amnesia patient."

"I can bring an extra pair of sheets and extra pillows up to your room so you're more comfortable," Reynar said.

"And we are refunding your stay," Einar added. "If another room opens up this week, you will be the first to know."

But Kilroy waved away the offers. "No worries. I get it. Shit happens."

Relief washed over the humans' faces.

"Is this alright with you?" Einar asked me. "I know that this is a...I know that you prefer to have the room to yourself this week..."

I thought about leaving. Einar was right. This week was about solitude. I wanted to be alone, not sharing a room with a peppy stranger. But if I left, where would I go?

"Actually..." I glanced at Kilroy, his eyes kind and open. "It'll be fine."

"Awesome!" Kilroy gave me a double thumbs up.

3
MAGNUS

I walked a line down the center of the room, sidestepping the coffin, as if I were taking a roadside sobriety test.

"It would be best if you kept your things on your side," I said to Kilroy once he returned to the room with his arms full of couch cushions. "Just to make things simpler."

"Simpler how?"

"We don't want our things to get mixed up. I don't know where you live. If I took something of yours by mistake, how would I get it back to you?"

"I can give you my address."

Now was not the time for logic. I continued walking the dividing line until I reached the wall.

"That should be even. It's a little tight, but we can make it work," I said. For a second, I missed the suite where Gunnar and I used to stay.

"So that's your side?" He pointed to where I was standing, conveniently by the window, covered with massive blackout curtains.

"Yes, since my suitcase is already here. And you can have all the space on your side. There's so much! *Kilroy-roy-roy-*

roy." I pretended to do an echo. It was corny, but no cornier than a double thumbs up.

"That works for me. But what if you have to take a piss?" he asked.

Behind him, on his side, was the entrance to the bathroom.

"One would hope that you wouldn't block me from using the lavatory."

"Just want to be sure of these rules." A playful twinkle lit up his eyes.

Was I frustrated that he was mocking me or that he looked this cute when he was mocking me?

"I'm trying to be fair and make the most of an awkward situation."

"What about the dresser?" He pointed to the ornate, sturdy piece of furniture behind me. "Since it's on your side of the room, am I not allowed to use it?"

"You don't strike me as someone who unpacks."

"And why's that?" Kilroy leaned against the wall and crossed his arms. Again with the playful twinkling of the eyes. What was so amusing about amicably splitting a room?

"The clothes on the floor, for one." I nodded at his shorts and what looked to be another Hawaiian shirt crumpled in a ball beside the coffin. "And you said that you slept on friends' floors. So one could assume…"

"Who is this 'one' person? Why don't you just say I?"

"Yes, we can share the dresser. Like I said, I am trying to make the best of an awkward situation."

"That's cool. Although I think all these rules are making things more awkward."

I got a slight rush when Kilroy crossed the line into my side of the room.

"Top or bottom?"

"Excuse me?" I felt my face turn red. It took a lot to make vampires blush, since blood was in short supply with us. "What kind of a question is that? If you must know, I'm versatile."

I didn't want to give him the satisfaction of making me flustered, so I thought I'd trip him up by being honest.

"I was talking about the dresser drawers. Did you want the top drawer or the bottom drawer?"

Shit.

I stammered, fully flustered. In my awkward silence, he chuckled with a face full of outright glee. Vampires were not meant to be this happy. We were meant to live in cold, dark places.

"It's all good, Magnus!" He clapped me on the shoulder. "Look, we're roommates for a week. Unexpected? Yes. But we can still enjoy our vacations. It's kinda fun having a roommate."

"How so?"

"We can chat about what we've been up to. Who wants to spend their vacation holed up alone in a hotel room?"

I did. That was my precise plan.

"You seem like you've been here a bunch, so you can share all the best things to do. I can save us a table for breakfast. It'll be great!" His two thumbs up sprang up as if on cue.

Kilroy made himself comfortable on his couch cushions. Seeing him sitting practically on the floor with little lumbar support sent a phantom pain up my own back.

Yes, vampires were immortal. But so was lower back pain.

"Why don't you sit at the desk?" I asked, pointing to the rolltop in the corner.

"It's on your side of the room."

"We can make an exception."

"Nah, I'm good here. These cushions are surprisingly comfortable!" He beamed with such positivity I had difficulty determining if he was bullshitting.

"Suit yourself." I finished the last of my unpacking and slid my suitcase in the luggage storage space under the coffin.

"I am so stoked to celebrate my first New Year's as a vampire. Okay, be honest. How crazy does it get up in here on New Year's Eve? Are we talking naked vampires hanging from the chandelier?"

Vampires had the ability to stand on the ceiling. Hanging from a chandelier seemed like a step down. That was what monkeys did.

"There are no New Year's Eve celebrations."

Kilroy's neck jutted out as if he had trouble hearing me. "What? No parties? New Year's is the biggest night of the year."

"Not for vampires. It's just...another night. There's nothing worth celebrating."

"I'd say making it to another year is worth celebrating. With champagne and hanging from chandeliers."

It seemed unnecessary and uncomfortable to hang from a light fixture whilst drinking a carbonated beverage, but perhaps things had changed in the human world since I'd been there.

"No vampire partakes in New Year's Eve festivities."

"But why?"

"I understand why humans celebrate the occasion. They only have so many good years in them. Each year that ticks away is another minute on the clock gone for good." I wiped away a speck of dust that had accumulated on the veneer of the coffin.

"Exactly! You gotta live life to the fullest!"

"But we are not humans. For us, the clock never stops ticking. It's pointless to celebrate a new year when you're immortal. What's another year in an endless eternity? It's but a tally mark on the interminable count of this afterlife, a sad reminder that we have all the time in the world. What happens when the thrill of flying like a bat and being nocturnal fades away, and you still have centuries of time on this godforsaken planet?"

I wasn't one for putting a positive spin on things. I had lost my ability to sugarcoat during the Great Depression. Being a vampire was a long, arduous, lonely slog through time. The sooner I burst Kilroy's perky bubble, the better off he would be.

"Cool." Kilroy nodded at what I said, but with a skeptical glint in his eye, the way a young adult would listen to the rants of their racist, out-of-touch grandparent. "I think maybe it's best that you take a nap. You're probably wiped from your trip. I'm going to scope out the premises."

He stood up and strolled to the door. I thought about saying something, perhaps taking back the severity of my statement, but lying would do no good. Being a vampire wasn't sexy and fun.

Relief hit me when he left the room. I could finally get my peace and quiet.

4

KILROY

Life was crazy. One minute, I was chilling on the beach in Hawaii, looking up at the moon. The next, this vampire came out of the bushes and chowed down on my neck. Oddly enough, getting bitten felt a lot like getting a hickey.

I didn't know what the heck Magnus was talking about. I'd only been a vampire for a few months, but so far, it was awesome. Sure, it was an adjustment.

This group of vampires found me after the bite, and they helped me adjust to my new life. They set me up in a sweet apartment and taught me how to use my new superhuman strength. (I had superhuman strength! Take that, Thor!) Apparently, a long time ago, all the vampires got together and decided to create a formal system for helping new vampires get on their feet. Maybe they weren't around to help Magnus and that was why he was being crustier than a stale piece of bread. I didn't blame them. The guy was kind of a downer. Where did he live when he wasn't at the Hotel Draugr? A trash can on Sesame Street?

I was a pro at making the best of things. In my human

life, I traveled the world with my best buds surfing the most righteous waves on the planet. Sometimes, the tides didn't go in our favor, or there was a massive storm, or sharks came around looking for a snack. But we rolled with it. We found ways to have fun even if we couldn't get in the water.

I'd have fun this week even though I was forced to room with a walking sad trombone.

And it didn't matter if the hotel didn't throw a New Year's party. I had other plans.

One of the many awesome things about being a vampire was that we couldn't freeze to death. We liked the cold. While I still preferred a warm beach, my distaste for snow and winter was gone.

I was able to trek through the mountains of Iceland wearing my go-to outfit: a Hawaiian shirt, cargo shorts, and flip-flops. I walked through the snow and down the mountain into an area filled with pine trees. I could feel the cold, but it wasn't painful, just uncomfortable. I probably should've brought a hoodie.

Another bonus about being a vampire: when I got tired of walking, I could turn into a bat and fly the rest of the way.

How could Magnus hate being a vampire when we had the freaking ability to fly? Batman couldn't fly, but we could.

I sailed through the air until I reached the Black Fortress.

Lava crystallized millions of years ago into mammoth black stone structures. I stared in awe at the craggy, spindly rocks, alone in the middle of barren terrain, jutting into the dark sky.

Currently, it was dormant, but not for long. In a few nights, the Black Fortress was going to be the most epic spot in Iceland. Nay, in the world!

I pulled a picture from my back pocket. It had been folded and unfolded so many times that there was a white line down the middle, but I could still make out everyone. Biff, Dirk, Amelia, Damian, and last but not least, human me, laying across their laps and giving the camera two big thumbs up. Behind us was the ocean waiting to be conquered. We'd gotten through an incredible surf with waves taller than skyscrapers. I faced down walls of crystal blue water and the most colorful fish swimming beneath me. It was a day I would never forget spent with guys (and a token girl) I'd never forget.

I kissed my finger and touched the photo. "See y'all soon."

I took my time getting back to my room and hoped that Magnus was asleep when I returned. I didn't need his negative vibes harshing my vacay.

Magnus was still up. Whomp whomp.

"Hey, is everything okay?" I asked when I saw him standing over my suitcase.

"Yes. Why would it not be?" He stepped aside and hung awkwardly by the desk. There wasn't much space in the room, so he only had so many options. "Kilroy, I hope you don't mind–"

I opened my suitcase to pull out clothes for sleeping, yet my sweats were missing. As were all my other clothes. "Uh, where's my stuff?"

Magnus opened the bottom dresser drawer.

"You unpacked my suitcase?"

"I did. That way, we can put your suitcase under the coffin and free up space in these tight quarters." Magnus looked at the floor for a second, like he was a little embarrassed by going this extra mile.

"Oh, good call." He even folded them. They were in better shape than when I packed them. I was a shove-everything-in-a-duffel-bag kind of packer.

"I figured since you're sleeping on the floor, it was the least I could do."

"Thanks," I said, actually touched. It should've been weird—I mean, the dude touched my underwear—but in the moment, I thought it was a sweet gesture. The stuff that might've seemed strange when I was human, I just rolled with now. He was offering a twig that had broken off from an olive branch. "Are you going to sleep?"

"Falling asleep is a process for me."

"Same." My mind had this annoying habit of thinking of a million random things as soon as I got into bed. "Maybe it's good that we're stuck being roommates. We can shoot the shit until we get tired."

"I suppose we can."

I noticed that Magnus was wearing silk pajamas this time. Was he self-conscious about sleeping in the buff with me around?

I changed into my sweatpants and thermal for sleep. I liked being warm when I slept. Then I brushed my teeth in the bathroom. Even in the afterlife, I had to worry about dental hygiene. Ugh. I heard that getting a cavity filled in my fangs was extraordinarily painful.

I sat on my makeshift bed with my back against the wall looking up at Magnus in the coffin. It was almost like bunk beds.

"Where did you go tonight?" he asked.

"Uh, nowhere. Just took a walk. And I flew a little. Do vampires say they took a flight when they turn into a bat?"

Magnus chuckled. "You're a brand new vampire. No more than three months old, yes?"

"Yeah. Like, exactly. How could you tell?"

"Because you're enthusiastic."

He said that like it was a bad thing.

"What can I say? Being undead doesn't bite." It was a shame I didn't live long enough to have kids because I've got dad jokes for days.

"I hope you've gotten those puns out of your system." Magnus shook his head, and a lock of his severely combed back honey-colored hair fell in his eyes.

"So that's how you could tell I was a new vampire? My jokes?"

He shook his head no. "It's because you still have your memories."

"You don't?"

"No. Neither do most vampires."

"Do you choose to forget because it's too painful?"

"I wish it were as poetic as that." A wry smile took over his face, showing off the mature creases of his forehead. "How many memories do you have from when you were a small child?"

"I have some."

"But not as many as you have as an adult, yes?"

"Yeah, I think." My childhood memories were weird. I had flashes of walking through the hallway of my best friend's house and gym in my elementary school, but I couldn't remember what my bedroom looked like.

"But when you were nine, you probably had a lot more memories of that time."

"Probably."

"That's because the farther away you get from a period in your life, the less memories you retain. You'll reach a point where you've been a vampire for so long that those memories of your human life fade away, as if they were memories of being a small child. One day, a century from now, when you reach into your brain for your earliest memory, it'll be of right now."

There was a time when my friends and I got high, and one of them rambled about his theory proving that God was scientifically real. It blew my mind in the same way my mind was blown now. Only this time, it was anything but cool. It was tragically uncool.

Time stopped for no one, not even vampires.

Would I forget my friends? Would I forget that time I got high and learned that God existed?

If I didn't have memories of my past, then who was I? No wonder Magnus was crabby.

"So you have no memories of being human?" It couldn't hurt to double-check.

"No."

"You don't remember anything about your old life? The house you grew up in as a child? Wild nights on the town with friends?" I gulped back a lump in my throat. "Your family?"

"Unfortunately not."

"You don't remember anything about them? Even what they look like?"

He shrugged. "I don't even remember what I look like."

Magnus said it in such an off-the-cuff way, it took me a moment to realize he wasn't joking.

"But how is that…" I clamped my eyes shut, the realization kicking me in the nuts. "We have no reflection."

"And we don't show up in photographs or videos."

"Because they only capture living things." I picked at a

stray thread on my lumpy pillow. "You didn't swipe a photo from your house after you were bitten?"

"Photographs didn't exist back then." He shrugged.

I was wrong. Being a vampire kinda did bite. I was going to be a guy who walked the earth for years and years and years with no family, no memory of the things that made me smile, and no way to check if I had a zit. Would I forget what the ocean looked like and smelled like?

"I'm assuming this isn't what you meant by shooting the shit." His forehead creased in concern.

I stared at the floor, trying to imagine what my life would look like in 100 years. 200 years.

"I used to surf," I said quietly. "I traveled with my ChoBros all around the world to hit the greatest waves. Maui. Australia. "

"Forgive me. I try to stay up on slang because I love to study language, but I'm not familiar with the term ChoBros."

I smiled wistfully. "That's because we made it up. ChoBros are my Chosen Brothers. I wasn't close with my family. I left home at eighteen and found my way into this group of surfers. They were the family I chose."

And I missed them so much it made my chest hurt. We were supposed to grow old together and be senior surfers. We were going to let a giant wave carry us into the sea forever. The plan wasn't for me to bite the big one at twenty-five. Or rather, have the big one bite me.

"There's nothing better than being out in the sun, under that big blue sky, for hours."

"Vampires can't be in sunlight or else we–"

"Burst into flames. I know, Magnus."

I ran my finger over my puka shell necklace. One benefit of having no reflection was that I couldn't watch myself lose my wicked tan. I closed my eyes and imagined the warm salty breeze hitting my face.

"My favorite part was getting up just before dawn to head out to the surf and watching the sunrise over the water. I saw the most beautiful sunrises. The sun peeking over the waves, ripples of pink and purple across the sky. Sunrises are the best."

Now they would have to live in my memories until I forgot them.

"Do you remember what a sunrise looks like?" I asked.

"I've seen pictures."

"Pictures. Man, pictures don't do it justice." I leaned against the wall and slumped down. I tried to hold onto memories, but what could I do besides clench my eyes shut? "I guess you're right, Magnus. Being a vampire is rough."

"Maybe you'll have better luck than me," he said, striking a hopeful tone. "Maybe you'll remember things. I didn't eat enough tuna fish as a human and it stifled my memory."

"Can vampires not eat tuna fish sandwiches?"

"We can. But then we get tuna fish breath and nobody wants to be near us."

I snorted a laugh.

"There has to be something you like about being a vampire," I said, practically pleading.

He thought on it for a moment. "I don't have to worry about sunburns anymore."

"That's one!" I played along, too. "I don't have to deal with people tagging me in bad photos online."

"You can save money on sunglasses."

"No more having to renew my driver's license."

"You can have a bad hair day and never even know it."

I combed a hand through my hair. "Am I having a bad hair day?"

"No. You look good. You're very attractive," Magnus said. "I mean...since you can't see yourself. Objectively, you are a very attractive man. You have...objectively attractive features."

Did a flash of heat just go up my back at Magnus calling me attractive? I was ladies only as a human, but I kept thinking about Magnus shirtless and his manly, barrel chest.

"You look good too, Magnus."

The dark cloud over my new life disappeared, at least temporarily. As long as I could still laugh, life would be okay.

"This could be a whole new era for me. I have a whole new lease on life," I said.

"Well, not life..."

"I was able to leap up half a mountain to get here. I leaped! All by myself! And I didn't even need to stretch."

The hotel was built into the mountain with no normal entrances for cars or pedestrians. That kept it secret and impenetrable from humans. It was a vampire lair. I was in a vampire lair!

"And my senses are heightened. Like I am getting hints of the most beautiful, fragrant scent that I've never smelled before. What is that?"

"It's snow."

"Snow smells this good? I thought it was wet and cold."

"That's how it smells for humans. We're able to smell its true, natural scent."

"Are you serious right now, Magnus? That is awesome! Dang, I thought being a vampire was cool before. But I didn't realize how kick-ass it was."

Magnus cracked a warm smile as his icy facade melted. I

had a feeling that this conversation was more fun than he'd had in a while. I could tell when people weren't having fun.

He held up a finger. "Also, you don't have to worry about infections. Say goodbye to the common cold."

"Sweet!" I held out my hand for a hi-five. "This is going to be the best week!"

"It's been quite a while since I high-fived someone. Back in the Sixties, there was a moment when vampires were obsessed with high-fiving people and wearing tie dye." Magnus cringed at the memory. "Tie dye wasn't a good look on the undead. Too many colors."

I fell back on my makeshift bed and laughed at the image of serious vampires decked out in tie dye. I laughed until my stomach hurt.

"Well, the sun is going to be coming up soon, so we could get to sleep. Are you sure you're going to be okay on the floor?"

"Yeah. I've slept on rocky beaches. This is the lap of luxury compared to that." I gave him my signature double thumbs-up.

"Great." Magnus responded with the more socially acceptable singular thumb up.

I lay down and stared at the ceiling, excited for the week ahead. I would use this time to explore my vampiredom, then cap it off with an epic New Years.

"Hey, Magnus, thanks for being cool about the room situation. I'll try and stay out of your hair so I don't ruin your trip. Have a good night."

"Day."

"What?"

"Vampires don't say 'have a good night.'"

"Right. Nocturnal." I snapped my fingers.

5

MAGNUS

The coffin was the very definition of hand craftsmanship. Built by artisans and carved with unique patterns, it blocked out all light and sound.

Well, most sound.

I awoke from a peaceful sleep to the sounds of my roommate tossing and turning. The floor creaked every time he moved. His elbow banged against the wall as he tried to maneuver into a good position. And then there was the muttering under his breath as the pillows slipped from under him. With my heightened senses, I could practically feel the discomfort seeping off him.

I tried to ignore it, but every time I was about to slip into a deep slumber, there was another *thunk* or *bonk* or muttered *dammit*. We might've been eternal, but we vampires needed our beauty sleep just as much as humans. Nobody wanted to be around a cranky vampire.

I pushed open the coffin case. My worst suspicions were confirmed. Kilroy looked miserable.

"Kilroy."

"I'm cool, Magnus. Just finding my sweet spot."

He had a better chance of finding the world's smallest needle in the world's biggest haystack.

"The pillows are a little slippery on the floor." He snapped his fingers. "Maybe if I put some clothes underneath, it can keep them in place."

He went to sit back, then rubbed at his neck with what looked to be a sudden crick. Most vampires were calm sleepers with their hands crossed on their chest. But new vampires didn't have it as easy: they were still used to sleeping on their side or their stomach. They had to learn a whole new sleeping position.

"Kilroy, I don't think that makeshift bed is sufficient."

"Nah. It's totes sufficient. Just needs some tweaking."

I let out a sigh. "Kilroy, why don't you join me in the coffin?"

"Are you sure?" A flash of relief crossed his face at the suggestion. "I don't want to interrupt your sleep."

"But you see, you already are."

"I can be quieter."

"Kilroy, get in the coffin." I rubbed at my eyes, heavy with sleep which could not come. "It's only fair. Just because this room was double-booked doesn't mean you have to suffer on the floor. There's enough room in here for both of us."

I immediately doubted that statement once it left my tongue, but it was too late to turn back.

"We can sleep head to toe," he said. His hair stuck up in back in an endearing case of bed head.

"We can't." The coffin narrowed at the end to keep feet snug. Unless Kilroy wanted to sleep with my feet in his mouth, then it was a non-starter.

"Are you–"

"Yes. I am absolutely certain. We can share." This coffin

was a single, but Kilroy and I were slim enough to make it work. Because of the tight dimensions, our bodies would be pressed close together, a thought that was causing a funny flutter in my stomach.

Kilroy stood up and shuffled to the coffin. He wore sweatpants and a thermal top, a stark contrast to my silk pajamas, which was itself a stark contrast to my preference for sleeping in the nude. His outfit was likely a holdover from his human life. The thermal outlined the curves of his muscles. The sweatpants left more to the imagination, and my imagination dared to wander.

Cease this at once, I told myself. *This vampire merely wants a place to sleep.* He didn't need a much-older vampire commenting on his attractiveness and lusting at the thought of sharing a coffin.

I scooched over as Kilroy climbed inside. The coffin was snug, but with another person in here, it was extra tight. We were sardines encased in fine craftsmanship.

There was no other place to move: Kilroy stretched his long, firm body flush against mine. We both squirmed to get comfortable, two puzzle pieces trying to fit. We quickly realized that it was impossible for us both to lie flat.

"Maybe you can lie flat and I can sleep on my side," Kilroy offered.

"Perhaps that could work."

Kilroy leaned against my prone body, warming up my left side. I detected a hint of a beachy smell from him. He'd ingested so much salt water and sand during his tenure as a surfer that they carried with him after death. It made me long for a piña colada.

"How's this? Are you comfortable?" Kilroy asked as he snuggled against me, his undead body pillow.

There was a problem: one part of me refused to play dead.

"I'm okay." My cock stirred, testing the strength of my pajamas. It'd been a long time since I shared a coffin with a man.

Kilroy's leg rubbed against mine as he got into position. It only caused my cock to swell more. If his hand moved in the wrong direction, we would have a very awkward encounter.

"Actually, I'm going to turn on my side. That will give us each the most amount of room." And by turning away from Kilroy, my cock could be as rock hard as it wanted without causing any disturbances.

I wasn't sure what my sexual orientation was as a human, but as a vampire, I was fully bisexual. Becoming unshackled from the social norms of human society allowed vampires the freedom to experience pleasure with whomever we wanted. While I didn't remember my own sexual awakening, other vampires confirmed the shift, saying it was like a weight lifted off them. As a result, most vampires were easy lays. We had all the time in the world; we might as well have fun with it.

"You still good?" Kilroy asked once we were both on our sides.

"Yes." My erection could rage in peace for a few more moments before calming down.

Or, I thought it would, but just as I was falling to sleep, Kilroy threw an arm around me and shuffled closer. His body, and especially his crotch, were flush against me.

Was he doing this on purpose or was he sleep-spooning?

I cleared my throat to wake him up.

"Sorry. My bad," he said groggily. He pulled his arm off me and shuffled an inch back, leaving my body cold. I was a vampire. I was supposed to be used to being cold. But being warm had its perks.

Unfortunately, I couldn't fall back asleep. I was in an unusual position and all too aware of the dead space between us. There was a man who was objectively very attractive sleeping an inch away from me.

"Hey, Magnus," Kilroy said a few minutes later. "This is going to sound weird, but could we try how we were, with my arm on you? I'm not used to sleeping on my side, and I think it might help me get some sleep tonight. Would it bother you?"

I brushed a hand against my crotch to confirm it was rock hard again.

"We can give it a try," I said in as lowkey a tone as I could muster considering I was apparently seconds away from humping the coffin wall.

"Sweet." Kilroy really went for it, smushing his body against mine and folding his arm over my body. He pulled me close to him. "Let me know if this is weird or uncomfortable."

It was very much both. But who said weird and uncomfortable had to be bad things?

6

KILROY

Uh...was I into dudes?

Something strange had been happening since I became a vampire. Well, aside from all the regular vampire stuff like turning into a bat, drinking blood, and sleeping in a coffin.

I had been finding myself, like...into dudes. I would check out other vampires, suddenly aware of their chests and their asses. And now with Magnus, I was going way beyond checking out. I was thinking about his body and how I wanted to taste it. I was actively stopping myself from giving into my urge to grope him in this coffin.

Was it weird?

It was weird.

But it didn't seem as weird as I thought it would. I mean, as a human, it would be weird and totally uncalled for. Yet in vampireland, there was this sense that anything goes. None of the vampires I met seemed judgmental. We were all stuck living forever, so we might as well do what we could to find a bit of happiness.

Even if that happiness involved blowing and fucking each other until we saw stars.

Dude.

"Like I said, just give me a holler if this is uncomfortable for you, and I can go back to sleeping on the floor. I really don't mind."

I was uncomfortable, but that was from contorting my hips so that my obvious hard-on didn't dig into my coffin-mate's ass.

Magnus did not seem like one of those anything goes vampires. He probably lived in Victorian times when everybody wore corsets and nobody had sex. Considering we had to spend a week sleeping like this and that he was one of the only vampires I knew, I had to keep my urges in check.

I stared at the back of his head while I tried to fall asleep, but that only made me want to nuzzle in his hair. I found a mark on the lid and focused there, kinda like when I used a urinal in a public bathroom.

After a few minutes, I could tell by his breathing that he was still awake.

"Hey, so like, do you ever miss being human?" I asked him. Was that a loaded question for drifting asleep? Possibly, but serious questions were made for the anonymity of the dark.

"I actually do not."

"You don't miss the human world?"

"No. I quite loathe it, to be perfectly honest."

"You do?" Loathe was a strong word.

"I have no interest in going back and being around humans," he said with a finality that took me by surprise. I thought it was a given that all vampires wanted to be humans again. "Humans are violent, malicious, unfeeling creatures. I want nothing to do with them."

His body tensed under my hand.

"Whoa. You really hate them. Do all vampires hate humans?"

In other words, would this be me one day, turning against my ChoBros and all the wonderful people from my human life?

"I can't speak for other vampires, but I assure you Kilroy, the feeling is mutual. Humans hate us. They have a biological need to kill us. We are an affront to their way of life."

"Not all humans. What about Einar?"

"Einar is descended from a special group of humans called conduits. They are able to see us as people, not creatures to be destroyed. But I assure you, people like him are a very slim minority. The vast majority of humans on earth detest us and show their true ugliness when they see us."

My nighttime chit-chat took an unexpectedly dark turn. Magnus remained tense, a coiled cat ready to attack. I felt bad for hitting a nerve. I massaged his shoulder and back with my spooning arm until I felt his breath return to calm.

"Maybe vampires and humans can coexist," I said.

"They can't."

"Sure, there are some bad humans, but there are probably bad vampires, too." The humans that I knew, my ChoBros, were good people. They loved everyone, no matter where they were from.

After a moment of silence, when I thought Magnus had fallen asleep, he began to speak.

"I used to come to the Hotel Draugr with Gunnar. We vacationed here every year in the last week of December. We stayed in this magnificent suite in a king-size coffin. We went skiing. We sipped coffee by the large windows and stared out at the moonlit volcanoes in the distance. Gunnar was up for anything. Every year when we checked in, he would step inside our suite, collapse on the couch, and say 'Let's live here!' Like clockwork."

"He sounds cool."

"He was the one who made sure I lightened up, that I learned to enjoy things."

"How long were you together?"

"Only ten years. But they were my favorite years."

I did a double take. Ten years was a long-ass time, but then I remembered that Magnus had been around for centuries. One decade was a drop in the bucket to him.

"Did you two break-up?"

"Gunnar was slayed, about three years ago," he said matter-of-factly. I wondered how many times he'd had to relay that news to others. "We were enjoying a nighttime spa in these natural hot springs outside Vancouver. That's when this ragtag group of vampire hunters came upon us."

"I'm so sorry, Magnus."

"Gunnar told me to run. He didn't hesitate. He distracted them while I escaped. I had heightened abilities and strength. I should've fought back."

"You were scared."

"I should've fought back."

My heart broke for Magnus. I wished there was something I could do to cheer him up, but what could I do? I couldn't bring Gunnar back. So I pulled him close, letting him know in this moment, he wasn't alone.

Also, I was a fan of *Buffy the Vampire Slayer* when I was human, but I would *not* be watching that show anymore.

"Such is undead life," he said. "There are vampire hunters around the world. Some of them even bring camera crews with them."

"But we can't show up on camera."

"I didn't say they were smart."

We let out a break of laughter that punctured the mood.

"I was a dumb human. I was drunk on the beach after an epic surf that day. My friends had all gone back to our place. This guy came up to me and asked if I had a light. Before I could find it odd that he'd asked someone who wasn't smoking, he bit me. I laughed as it was happening, that's how wasted I was. But it all worked out because now I get to share this uncomfortably small coffin with you."

"Dracula sacrificed himself so we could be double-booked at a hotel."

I burst out laughing. Magnus had a dry sense of humor that could be straight-up savage.

We settled back into silence. I remained very aware of his body against mine. The rise and fall of his breath helped to lull me to sleep.

"Hey, Magnus," I whispered.

"Yes?"

"I know we're stuck sharing this tiny-ass coffin, but I'm having a really good vacation so far."

"Against all odds, I think I am, too."

7

KILROY

I woke up the next morning in an empty coffin, the extra space feeling like a gulf of dead air without Magnus. Cold air hit my chest.

I lifted the coffin door and found Magnus sitting at the desk on what seemed to be an important phone call. He was all business...except for the pajamas. Had I really slept through him waking up? I hadn't slept that well since I became a vampire. The whole nocturnal thing was throwing off my circadian rhythms. Yet I emerged from the coffin refreshed.

"Morning," I said, stretching my arms out for a yawn.

"Evening," Magnus corrected. "Mornings are for mortals."

"Catchy. You should embroider that on a pillow."

I descended from the coffin, stretching my legs and arms.

"Now that I'm a vampire, I kicked my coffee addiction," I said.

"Well, that makes it all worth it then." Magnus cocked an eyebrow, looking amused and, uh...sexy?

I scratched my head and sensed that I had a wicked case of bedhead. Like, we were talking finger-in-light-socket height. Man, I could really go for a mirror right now.

"How'd you sleep?" he asked. "I hope things weren't uncomfortable for you."

"Nope." His body against mine was more effective than any sleeping pill. "Are you on a call?"

"I'm checking with Einar to see if there are any last-minute room cancellations. Maybe one of the guests was slayed or accidentally stayed up too late and got caught in daylight."

"Cool. Well, not cool for them."

I couldn't help but feel a little wounded. I knew it was tight quarters, and he seemed like a guy who wanted his space, but I thought we made the best of an awkward situation. All things considered, it was a nice night.

At least, I thought it was. Maybe Magnus was crawling out of his skin the entire time. Shit, what if my boner accidentally brushed against him last night—er, day?

Magnus pointed at the phone. "He's double-checking with Reynar."

I crossed my fingers that Einar was still all booked up. And that no vampires had died overnight.

I flicked my eyes over to Magnus. He pushed up his sleeve to itch his arm, revealing his strong forearms streaked with a thick row of hair. I resisted the urge to gawk.

I was into hairy forearms now? I'd dig into that later. For now, I snuck another ogle.

"I see. And you're sure?" Magnus said into the phone. "Okay. Well, thank you for checking." He hung up the phone. "We're out of luck."

"Shoot," I said, willing myself to sound let down by the news. "That's okay."

"Unfortunately, it is what it is. But I'll keep checking with Einar."

"Sounds good," I said with all the conviction of a bad actor reciting lines from an even worse script.

I strode past Magnus into the bathroom to brush my teeth. At first, it was weird being in a bathroom without a mirror, but then I realized that I didn't need one to brush my teeth. It wasn't as if I had trouble finding my mouth.

What was odd were the metal rods running across the ceiling.

"Are these towel racks?" I asked.

Magnus peeked his head into the bathroom. "Those are for hanging."

"Hanging what?"

"Yourself." He pointed to the metal rods also present in our bedroom. I must've missed them when I checked in. I was focused on the sweet coffin.

"I'm confused," I said.

"Many vampires like to hang upside down to sleep or just because they want to."

"Oh. Like bats, right?"

"Precisely. All rooms in the hotel have them."

Interesting. Being a vampire was endlessly fascinating, I thought as I pressed a glob of toothpaste onto my brush.

"So what are you up to tonight, Magnus?" I asked through my foamy mouth.

"Probably relaxing. Maybe going to the observation windows with a cup of blood-infused hot chocolate and looking out at the moon and stars."

Magnus got dressed in the room. I kept my gaze inside the bathroom, staring at the painting hanging where a mirror should be, a recreation of that famous shot of Adam and God touching fingers like *E.T.*

"Sounds very zen," I said of his plans. "Do you ever worry that you're going to run out of things to think about?"

"How is that possible?"

"You've been a vampire for centuries. What if you run out of deep thoughts?" I washed out my mouth and felt the minty tingle on my tongue.

"I doubt that is possible."

I peeked my head out and shrugged. Magnus was fully dressed in an identical outfit from yesterday: black pants, a crisp white shirt, and his wool coat.

"What about you?" he asked. "I take it you'll want to do something more engaging."

I wasn't sure if that was a backhanded compliment or not. I planned to wing it in Iceland until New Year's Eve, but that would probably get an eye roll from Magnus.

"I have some fun ideas. I think I'm going to go into town, do some window shopping."

He turned serious. "Be careful down there. Make sure not to go down until after midnight so you don't risk running into humans."

"I know. I got the same brochure at check-in as you." According to said brochure, the town at the bottom of the mountain had a quaint main street that closed down by six o'clock. It was deserted at night, likely a function of the townspeople having an inkling about the hotel. There were some vampire-run shops and restaurants, marked on the handy map in the brochure, that stayed open overnight.

"I know how to be safe in public." I cocked a bratty eyebrow at him.

"It's different. Stick to the shadows. Just be careful. Be smart. Be safe." The concern in Magnus's voice and demeanor caught me by surprise. It stopped our playful banter in its tracks.

"I'll be careful." I gave him a solemn nod.

"Good." He exhaled. "Are you finished in there?"

"Almost. I just have to wash my face."

"You can't get acne as a vampire. Blemishes cannot grow on our skin."

"I'm not a teenager. I don't get acne. I like to wash my face because it helps wake me up." Although his forearms were doing a heck of a job at that. "We can both squeeze in."

"I don't know about that. The coffin is tight, but the bathroom is a shoebox."

"Magnus, we're vampires! We can make it work." I turned myself upside down and hooked my feet under the rods on the ceiling. "You obviously never played Tetris."

I spit my toothpaste foam into the sink. Hanging upside down made it much easier. Score!

Magnus tried to resist, but his lips lifted in a reluctant smile as he stepped inside. That, more than hanging upside down, gave me a rush of blood (or whatever was inside me) to the head.

8

MAGNUS

The observation deck was on the top floor of the hotel. Oversized rocking chairs and rocking loveseats overlooked the mountain range with a picturesque view of the night sky. Vampires got to take advantage of views that humans could only dream about.

On both sides of me, the rocking loveseats were occupied by couples. To my right was a sweet couple holding hands. To my left was a couple making out like they were in the backseat of their convertible parked on Lovers Lane. The sounds of their fangs clinking together echoed in the night air.

I wondered what Kilroy was up to in town. Was he having fun? Did he find a watering hole that was open to vampires?

It'd been years since I went into town. Gunnar and I had a scare there. Some punk kids spotted us walking down the street holding hands, their initial looks of terror coalesced into violence. Before they got any smart ideas, Gunnar and I hightailed it out of there, leaping to the roof of a nearby building until they were gone.

Was Kilroy having the same trouble? Despite our conversation last night, I had the feeling he didn't quite believe me about the threat of the living.

He was a friendly, sweet guy. If he saw a group of humans, he'd probably want to join them for a drink, not even thinking that they were capable of driving a stake through his heart.

Two thumbs down.

"He's fine," I said under my breath. "The kid can handle himself."

I strummed my fingers on my lap and ignored the moaning coming from the horndogs to my left.

The path into town was confusing. Einar had tried to map it in the brochure, but he didn't truly know the best path. What if Kilroy got lost? It wasn't like he could freeze to death, but nobody liked being lost, dead or alive.

And maybe the town had changed since the last time I was there. What if humans were staying out later? Or what if Kilroy got drunk and got into a bar fight with vampires? I heard one time, two vampires got into a fight and one staked the other in a fit of rage.

Was it possible for anyone to get enraged by my sweet, goofy vampire roommate?

I stood up and adjusted the lapel of my coat. It was my duty as an elder vampire to check up on newbies.

One jaunt down the confusing path later, I found myself on the main thoroughfare in town. It was a blast from the past, like visiting one's hometown and everything had changed. The lampposts were still wrapped with festive lights, but the newspaper dispensers and pay phones on the curb were gone, replaced with electric vehicle charging stations. The barrel trash cans were out, and in their place were mailbox-looking black cans that were solar-powered trash compressors. Anything solar-powered around here was a dicey proposition.

A few vampires stared into the front windows of the stores, most of which were different from what I remembered. The town even had a Starbucks. Groups of vampires stumbled out of speakeasies; Kilroy wasn't with any of them.

I strolled down the street, finding myself hit with the festive feeling. This was a lovely quaint town. Perhaps I should come more often. I kept my eyes peeled for Kilroy.

When he didn't show up on the main thoroughfares, I walked down every side street and peeked my head into every vampire-run establishment. I told myself I wasn't checking up on him, but when I found him, I was grateful I did.

He crouched in an alley with a wide-eyed ravenous stare possessing his cool blue eyes. He hid behind a dumpster and kept a watchful, hungry eye on the entrance to a new club where drunk humans stood outside smoking cigarettes.

The familiar low growl of a vampire on the hunt emanated from his mouth.

"Don't even think about it," I whispered, putting a firm hand on him and jolting him out of his stare.

9

KILROY

"What the fuck happened?" I asked Magnus.

He pushed a glass filled with a red concoction my way. "Drink."

If a Dirty Shirley Temple was a real drink, this would be it. The cocktail was dark red liquid topped with a cherry. This was my second drink of the night.

Magnus had taken us to a vampire speakeasy located underneath a bank. The entrance was an unassuming maintenance closet, where we had to utter a secret password to a huge vampire bouncer. The smoky, dark vibe was a stark contrast to the bright, sterile furnishings of the bank above ground. Not gonna lie: I felt like a total badass being here.

I downed most of the glass in a few expert chugs. Fortunately, my beer-chugging skills made the transition to my vampire life. The drink hit the spot and helped return me back to earth.

"I'll order you another," Magnus said.

"A third? I think I'm fine."

Magnus's eyes told me there was no negotiation here.

"He'll take another," he told the waitress, whose hair was

as spiky as her fangs. He pushed the rest of my remaining glass toward me. "Drink up."

I did as ordered. A burp slipped out when I was finished.

"I really think I'm good."

"You'll have another. It's on me. I'm glad I found you in time." Even though I was fine now, Magnus's face was still etched with concern.

"I don't know what the hell happened. I was having a lovely evening in town, and then something came over me… I wanted to feast."

"Your blood sugar was low."

"Huh." I looped my finger around the rim, picking up the last drops of my drink. "I thought that was a human thing."

"It means something different for us. We need to drink blood to survive."

"Obviously. That's Vampire 101."

"Do you know why, though? Blood has key nutrients for us. If you go too long without consuming it, your blood sugar gets low. Your body starts to obsessively crave blood, and it will do anything to get those nutrients."

"Like staking out some clubbers for a snack."

"Precisely."

I nodded at Magnus's drink sitting in front of him, the glass half-full.

"You drink up, too," I said.

He humored me with a sly smile before drinking up. A Magnus smile was extra rewarding because he seemed like a guy who rarely did it. His smiles were like sea turtles that only showed up on the shore once every five years.

"Make sure you have some blood everyday so you don't wind up in this situation again. Vampire cuisine has improved dramatically. There are now several kinds of meals and beverages that are 'blood-infused.'"

I had to laugh. "Is it strange to you that we're talking about drinking blood like it's no big deal?"

"No."

I couldn't imagine having this conversation as a human without getting tons of side-eye. But the thought of consuming blood didn't sound gross to me. It made my stomach rumble.

"You always want to be prepared," Magnus said. "In the Nineteenth Century, there was this pack of vampires who were on a camping trip. They forgot to pack enough blood with them, and when they turned ravenous, they came upon this human family traveling in a covered wagon and devoured them all. That poor Donner family never saw them coming."

The waitress brought over drink number three. I found myself getting a little tipsy. The fun kind of tipsy that bubbled under my skin, where all I wanted to do was laugh and smile, no matter what was said.

"Hey, Magnus. I have a question for you."

"You've had a myriad of questions since you met me. Why should this one be any different?"

I laughed, unsure if that was a joke. "Can vampires get drunk off blood?"

"Yes. Too much blood can mimic the effects of libations. Light-headedness, lowering of inhibitions."

Check and check.

"So, Magnus." I leaned forward and sloppily rested my chin in my hands. I stared into his magnetic gray eyes. "How many people have you bitten?"

He exhaled a heavy sigh. "Five."

"That's...not bad considering how old you are."

He arched an eyebrow. Apparently, immortal people could still be sensitive about their age.

"I mean, how...stately you are?" I bit my lip, then sipped my drink.

"It's not something I take lightly," he said. "When you bite someone, you're taking their life."

"But you're making them immortal."

"It's not the same. You're permanently altering it. Being a vampire isn't some big party."

"It can be! You just need the right playlist."

Magnus had zero reaction to my joke, which meant it bombed hard. Did the guy even know what a playlist was?

"When you're a human, you have a future to look forward to. You have urgency. Life is short." He spun his glass on the table, letting the condensation form a circle. "When I took a life, it was out of protecting myself or sheer desperation."

He removed a piece of paper from his wallet. It was old and crumpled, the edges turning to dust. He slid it over, and I put my tipsiness on pause to handle it delicately.

The five tally marks scrawled on the paper humbled me. A human life boiled down to a line.

"I keep that as a reminder," he said.

I folded it with the utmost care and slid it back. "Thank you for sharing this."

"You always want to stay hydrated. Never let yourself go more than two or three days without blood. There are haunts like these in most cities or underground butchers who supply product to vampires. Most vampires carry around a flask. Don't be one of those reckless vampires who goes out hunting."

He slipped the paper into his wallet.

"I won't." I put my hand on his and massaged it with my

thumb. I was a little blood-drunk and a little bisexual, but something else compelled me, a deep need to let Magnus know how grateful I was to be here with him.

I held up my glass. "Cheers."

"What are we cheersing to?"

"To being vampires." I kept my eyes on him as we clinked and drank.

10

MAGNUS

I tried to limit myself with blood cocktails, but Kilroy and I kept talking and kept ordering. I soon found myself intoxicated, in more ways than one.

Kilroy asked me lots of questions about the hotel. He wanted to know everything about the history, about Einar's family, about fun things to do, about hotel regulars. It turned out, I'd accumulated a mountain of knowledge about this hotel over my years coming as a guest. A cache of anecdotes had been stored in my brain and was waiting to come out.

I shared tales of Nosferatu himself staying here, of a wild party where one of the guests had stolen from a blood bank, of watching someone get so blood-drunk that they tripped over an extension cord and tumbled into broad daylight. Just because we were undead didn't mean we'd forgotten how to have a good time.

Kilroy ate up every story, his face glowing with glee. There was pure joy radiating from him, which wasn't something you normally saw with vampires. We were a more solemn bunch. After all, walking the earth for an eternity wasn't exactly living our best lives.

And perhaps this was the libation altering my brain, but it seemed as if...I had a suspicion that...it might be within the realm of possibility that...Kilroy was flirting with me?

After our fourth round, he got up and joined my side of the booth. He claimed he was having trouble hearing me. His musk flitted up my nose. The mood lighting caught his smile perfectly.

"So Magnus, you've been around a while. You must have all the dirt on historical figures."

"Just because I was around for hundreds of years doesn't mean I was present at all major historical events. I'm not Forrest Gump."

"You've seen *Forrest Gump*?"

"Of course. I do own a DVD player." I was old, not a luddite.

"What was it like being a vampire during the Roaring Twenties?" His eyes lit up with curiosity. They were as blue as the oceans he'd never surf again.

"It was...it was fun. There was this vampire who owned a grand estate on an abandoned island in the Bermuda Triangle. He threw lavish parties. Music, fireworks, exquisite cuisine. He would perform this trick where he stacked champagne glasses in a pyramid seven-feet-high, then pour sparkling blood on the top one. It would cascade to the bottom row."

"That sounds awesome!"

"Yes, well a conduit who was friends with some attendees gossiped about the party to his friend Scott Fitzgerald, who blatantly ripped it off for his hackneyed piece of tripe."

"Bummer. I think I read that book in high school. Well, I think I watched YouTube summaries on it, but told my teacher I read it." He smiled with his tongue sneaking between his front teeth, a move that made me even more light-headed. "What about the Great Depression? Was it depressing for vampires?"

"Yes. There were humans who for some reason blamed vampires for the economic crash. They were angry, and they needed a scapegoat. They hunted us. That was when organized vampire hunting organizations formed. I heard stories of slayers tying vampires' legs so they couldn't turn into a bat. They would attach rocks to their feet and throw them into the ocean."

"They drowned them?"

"But vampires don't die."

Kilroy's face surged with horror. "Are they still down there?"

It wasn't something I wanted to think about. But it was all the more reason to stay away from humans. They were experts in cruelty. At least when vampires bit a person's neck, we were doing it out of necessity.

"I apologize."

"For what?" Kilroy asked.

"Once again, I have brought the mood down." I didn't mean to be a downer. Somehow, my conversations always seemed to lead there. I wouldn't be surprised if Kilroy wanted to ditch me for jollier vampires.

"Not even! This is good stuff to know," he said.

"Perhaps this explains why I am lacking in the social department."

"If it makes you feel better, so am I."

I raised my eyebrows, highly doubting his assertion.

"It's true," Kilroy said. "I was kinda shy as a human. It wasn't until I found my ChoBros that I finally had a circle of friends, and even then, they did most of the socializing."

"I can't imagine you being shy."

"Believe it, bloodsucker." He tilted his head back and emptied the contents of his glass into his mouth. "I had this habit of overthinking things. My friends were really funny, and I always ran things to say through my head once or twice before saying them. But by that time, the conversation shifted to a new topic, so I wound up not saying anything."

He gave a modest shrug, but I could tell that was tough to admit for him.

"What about you? Were you social as a human?"

I held up my hands in the classic "I don't know" gesture.

"Right. You don't remember. Well, what about as a vampire?"

"Not particularly. I prefer peace and quiet." Getting close to someone meant I had to risk losing them. We lived in a world where we could be killed by sunlight or humans, two of the most abundant resources on earth. At least solitude didn't come with loss.

"Peace and quiet is cool. But so is the hum of being around people. Wait, come here a sec." Kilroy beckoned me to lean over. It made my heart jump for a second.

"What is it?"

"You got a little something on your lip." Kilroy wiped his thumb over the crest of my top lip, a simple, confident gesture that sent a tidal wave of excitement rushing through my veins. His thumb was slow and deliberate, his eyes never leaving mine. I was left with maximum goosebumps. I resisted every urge in my body to pull his thumb into my mouth.

He held up his thumb, a smear of red across the pad. "You had a little something."

"Oh." Was I blushing? It was times like these when I wished I could see my reflection.

Then Kilroy did something that set off a four-alarm fire in my chest: he licked his thumb.

"I thought you didn't like coming into town." He took the cherry from his empty glass and placed it on his tongue.

"I, uh. Yes, into town." I had to stop looking at his mouth. It was giving me all the wrong ideas. "I haven't been in town in a while, but I forgot how lovely and quaint it is. I should come back more often."

He plucked the cherry from the stem, and it made a little *pop* sound that sent a tingle down my spine.

"It's super cute. It reminds me of these small beach towns." Kilroy sucked the stem from his fingers and swirled it around in his mouth.

"The stem isn't edible."

He nodded that he understood, but obviously speech was out of the question. I also lost the ability to speak when I watched him pull the stem from his mouth, tied in a knot.

"Sweet! I still got it!" He proudly held up the knotted stem.

"You've established that you know multiple ways to play with your food. Congratulations," I deadpanned, even though inside, I was tied in a knot myself.

I took a sip of my drink to cool down.

"I wasn't sure if I could still do that, but I'm glad to say my tongue still works as a vampire."

And then I choked on my drink, the burn of liquid hitting my nose.

*Kilroy's tongue…*I couldn't let myself finish that sentence.

"What are you up to now? Should we head back to the room?" he asked.

I did not trust myself to return to the room at this moment, not in the aftermath of witnessing the skills of Kilroy's tongue.

"Have you ever been to the top of a volcano?" I asked while catching my breath.

"Like for real?"

"Correct."

"Uh, no. Is that a thing?"

"If by thing, you mean an activity we're able to do, then yes. It is a thing."

"Nice. Do I need a jacket? It must be extra freezing up there."

"We can adjust to colder temperatures." I clapped him on the shoulder. "And what's going to happen? We're going to freeze to death? We're already dead!"

11

MAGNUS

Even though I'd been coming to the Draugr Hotel for decades, I had only been volcano hopping once, my first year. Back when I wanted to try everything. Oh, youth.

Volcano hopping was popular among guests since we had multiple volcanoes to choose from. This was Iceland, after all. There wasn't actual hopping involved, though some vampires had tried.

During one of my bat flights to the hotel, I had discovered a squat-looking volcano. It wasn't as tall and mighty as the others in the country, but to me, it had a sense of pride that I connected with. It was confident in its lack of height and offered a stunning view of the ocean.

"This is wild." Kilroy walked along the rim of the volcano as if he were on a tightrope. He didn't have to hold out his hands for balance. He peeked inside. "Shit, that's deep!"

"Well, it is a volcano." I remained perched on a thicker part of the rim, letting my legs hang over the side. Clouds and stars floated around us.

"What happens if a vampire falls in?"

"They should be able to use their strength to leap out."

"What if it's too steep?" Kilroy pretended to do a roadside sobriety test, touching his nose with alternating hands.

"Then I guess they'll have to wait."

"For what?"

"For the volcano to explode and push them out."

"That could take millions of years."

I shrugged. "It's not like we don't have the time."

Kilroy covered his eyes and balanced on one foot. Now he was just showing off. "I'm surprised you came here then. You seem way too cautious to hang out on the rim of a volcano."

"This is one of the shallower volcanoes. We'll have no problem getting out." Gunnar once said that I was the only vampire obsessed with death.

"Whoa. Did you see that?" Kilroy pointed to the ocean in the distance, where whales peeked from the water, their fins silhouetted in the moonlight. "You can't get views like this when you're a human."

"What about from an airplane?"

"Nah. From an airplane, everything looks like ants. This is like a front row seat to nature."

That made me feel better. I'd never been on one. I was bitten before they were invented, and I couldn't board one as a vampire. I'd never make it through an airport unstaked.

Kilroy howled at the moon, a dead man full of life. "Man, there's so much I want to do now. I want to go everywhere. I want to scale the tallest mountains and trek across Antarctica and jump off the tallest waterfalls."

"We can still break our bones. We won't succumb to our injuries, but we will be in immense pain."

"You know what I really want to do? I want to surf at midnight. I remember late night surfs with my crew." Kilroy balanced on the volcano rim as if he were surfing, his legs swaying to find balance amid the imaginary waves. "Only the moon as a guide."

Vampires weren't known for surfing. We were more of an indoor species, like cats. Tropical climates that were known for their surfing were also known for being very sunny.

"I want to take on the waves that I couldn't master. I want to surf in ice water. There are probably great waves around here or in Greenland or the North Pole, but nobody could give it a try because the water was too freezing."

Surfing at the North Pole? The image brought a smile to my face. Santa Claus could never. It was a wild thought, but I assumed it wasn't outside the realm of possibility.

But mostly, I admired how upbeat Kilroy was. It was irritating at first, but his optimism was burrowing inside me. I was starting to wonder what I could do that I hadn't tried. Could this very old dog learn new tricks?

"I've heard of people swimming with dolphins. What if we swam with whales?" I offered. My suggestion paled in comparison to his ideas, but Kilroy lit up like a fireworks celebration.

"That. Sounds. Awesome. Maybe we could live inside a whale like Pinocchio."

"I don't think it'd be like the cartoon." Could vampires survive being swallowed by a whale? The real question was *Would we want to?* "Maybe you could teach me to surf."

"I can give you your first lesson right now."

I thought it was a joke, but Kilroy motioned for me to join him on the rim. He wasn't letting it go.

"Let's go, Magnus Moriarty."

My full name slid off his tongue in a low growl. It was, as the younger vampires would say, freaking *hawt*.

"How did you know my surname?"

"I sneaked a peek at your luggage tag."

I wondered what made him do that. Moriarty wasn't my real surname. I had picked it up somewhere in the late 1800s when *Sherlock Holmes* was first published. I was a fan, and I thought it'd be transgressive to name myself after the villain.

Kilroy had me stand on the rim. Even though I'd been here plenty of times, it was the first time when I actually stood on the edge of the volcano. I peeked into the abyss of darkness, heart palpitations building in my chest.

It's a shorter than average volcano, I told myself. *You have the superstrength to leap out. This is not the time to chicken out in front of Kilroy.*

The hard rock border dug into my feet, but I found my balance, my posture stick straight.

"Sweet. Now you need to anticipate the wave. Keep your knees bent slightly."

Kilroy demonstrated with intense focus. His body swayed with changes in the wind. He held his arms out for balance. He might've been on top of a volcano in the freezing Icelandic wilderness, but in his mind, he was on the surf riding one heck of a wave.

"Your legs and your core are most important." He rubbed a hand over his stomach. Did he think I didn't know what a core was or was he wanting to draw attention to his abs? Or maybe both? "You want to keep your core tight."

He bobbed his head around to avoid the imaginary brush of the waves. "Oh, now here comes a big one. Are you ready, Magnus?"

"I suppose so?"

A gust of actual wind picked up, and we really did have to keep our balance to stay up.

I had all the coordination of those inflatable men flailing

around in car dealership lots. If there was a tiny chance that Kilroy was attracted to me, it was vanishing right now.

"Good," he said with less confidence than I'd hoped.

"You're just saying that. I don't want to wipe out and fall into a volcano."

"Yeah. That'd suck. Your core isn't stabilized."

"How do I stabilize my core?" All I could think was to suck in my gut.

"Pretend that there's a piece of string tied to your belly button, and it's pulling backward to your spine."

"That sounds incredibly painful."

"Here." Despite us surfing on a razor-thin volcano edge, Kilroy managed to shuffle behind me. It was a tight squeeze, just like our coffin.

I liked tight squeezes. It was becoming our thing.

He wrapped an arm around my stomach and lightly pressed. "Flex these muscles."

"I don't have abs."

"I don't care about abs. I care about your abdominal muscles, which everyone living or undead has." He pulled me harder against him, pressing me like the world's luckiest orange.

I flexed my abdominals, pretending I had a wall of steel under my shirt. Fake it til you make it, right? It was minus twenty degrees out here and the wind wasn't helping, but all I could feel was his heat, fiery embers of his essence seeping through my clothes into my skin.

I bit back a moan. I bit back another when his breath danced on my neck.

"Very good," he said, his voice deep and raspy. "Stay tight."

At that moment, I wanted him to stretch me.

"Close your eyes," he commanded. "You're running a

massive tailpipe off the coast of Melbourne. The wave is curling and you only have one shot to take it before it takes you."

I leaned into his touch, my ass hitting his crotch, a million dirty thoughts running through my head. Dirty thought #1: I wanted this man touching me at all times.

"The tide is picking up," I whispered.

"We're on top of it. Look around, Magnus." He pulled me flush against him, the vibrations of his chest stirring in my loins. "Look at the height of the wave. A wall of water. We're riding it. We're doing it."

I pictured crystal clear water shooting up around us as we cut a path under the tropical sun. "We're doing it."

I didn't know what I was doing. My body was on another plane, riding this wave of heat. I grabbed his hand that was over my stomach, interlocking our fingers together. Then I moved us south. Destination: my raging erection.

Kilroy pulled his hand away just before we crossed my belt. He stumbled back and leaped high in the sky winding up at the opposite end of the volcano rim, as far away as geometrically possible.

Wipe out.

12

KILROY

What the hell was that? Magnus interlocked our fingers because he was scared. And what did I do? I moved our hands down to his crotch. Magnus didn't put up any resistance, but that was because he was scared and not sure how to surf. He was trusting me, and all I could think about was dick.

I had to pull it together. Magnus seemed like my first actual friend I'd made in this new life.

"Nice job," I said, shouting across the chasm. It was the first time I'd ever seen a purely awkward, uncomfortable look cross his refined face. "You're a natural."

"Thanks. If I ever go surfing, I'll remember what you said about the core," he shouted back.

"One sec." I squatted down then leapt over the gap to Magnus's side of the rim. (Vampire Plus: I could do an actual superhero leap and pose!) I cupped my hand on his waist to keep his balance. I didn't need my theatrics to cause Magnus to fall into a volcano.

"That's better."

"It's getting late. Don't want to be caught in the sun," he said.

The sky was pitch black. I couldn't imagine the sun would be that close to rising. But I didn't need to know proper sunrise times to know what he actually meant. Our fun evening was over. I had crossed a line.

"Right. No sun for us. Or else we perish, and that would..."

"Don't say that."

"Suck!" I gave him two thumbs up. "Hey, sorry about before. My hand slipped as we were pretend surfing. I don't want you to think..."

"Of course not! When it comes to surf lessons, you are a consummate professional. I think my hand slipped, too."

"It was a rocky surf out there." I appreciated that he didn't want me to feel bad. He was the consummate vampire.

"Ready to fly back?" he asked.

"Race ya!"

Magnus narrowed his eyes at me. "You're on."

In a snap, we turned into bats and zipped through the landscape.

I was fast. I'd always been fast. I was a sprinter in high school. That served me well as a bat, too. I pushed myself to flap my wings and speed through the mountains. But Magnus was putting up a fight. He kept up with me, his wings singing beside mine.

And then he dropped.

I didn't know where he went until I heard the buzzing below me. He was flying low, dodging and swerving through trees and hovering over the snowy terrain. I'd never seen a bat fly that low. His ability to dart around objects was stunning. It was like watching an Olympic athlete at the top of his game. He must've perfected his flying over his vampire lifetime.

He beat me to the hotel by nearly a full minute, and I was happy to take the L. I was in the presence of greatness.

MAGNUS GOT into the coffin to go to sleep first.

"Is this still cool?" I asked, pointing to the empty space beside him.

"Yes. We've already established that the couch cushions don't work for you."

"Sweet."

The coffin shook as I climbed inside. Magnus's heat enveloped me as soon as our bodies made contact. I shut the lid, shrouding us in pitch black darkness.

"Is it alright if we switch positions tonight?" Magnus asked, letting my mind travel to very dirty places.

"Yeah, sure. That's cool." It was for the best, as I worried I'd have to contort myself to hide my boner again.

I turned to the coffin wall. Magnus wrapped his arm over me, and I sunk into his embrace. I reminded myself that I wasn't supposed to enjoy this. We were sleeping together out of necessity.

Correction: We were sleeping beside each other, not sleeping together.

"I never thought I'd like sleeping in a coffin," I said. "I hated confined spaces as a human."

"It's an instinct that's acquired when you become a vampire."

"Kinda like how cats love hanging out in boxes."

"Precisely."

He snuggled against my body.

"Well, have a good day," I said. "That still sounds weird even though it's factually accurate."

"You, too." Magnus shuffled to get comfortable, creating friction against my back and my ass. "You seem tense."

"Sorry. Just getting comfortable." I exhaled a breath and wiggled myself into my regular position. I allowed myself to sink into his embrace, his warmth lulling me to sleep.

"Hey Magnus," I said into the darkness. "I had fun tonight."

"As did I. Kilroy, I had a question for you."

"I'm all ears."

"How did you wind up coming to Iceland? For someone who loves the ocean, I'm surprised you found yourself here."

"I'd always wanted to come to Iceland. In the human world, it's become a trendy destination. Kind of like the avocado toast of vacation spots. So I had to see what all the fuss was about."

"I like to stay abreast of happenings in human culture, but for the life of me, I do not understand the obsession with avocado toast."

"Humans are weird."

We shared a chuckle, then I listened as Magnus fell into the rhythmic breathing of sleep.

A sharp pang of guilt hit my chest. I had just lied to my first real vampire friend. I was never the kind of guy who lied to friends.

But if Magnus found out I came to Iceland to hang out with my ChoBros, he would never talk to me again.

The ChoBros were my family. It would be a shock for them to see me, but our love for each other would triumph.

And when it did, I could introduce them to Magnus, and he'd see that we could coexist with humans.

It was best that I kept Magnus in the dark for now.

I heaved out a tense breath. It would all work out in the end because things always worked out in the end.

Right?

13

MAGNUS

As part of the special skills that come with being a vampire, we possessed the ability to move quietly when needed, such as when sneaking up on a fresh neck or partaking in a surprise party. Vampires could move in the shadows, our feet light as feathers.

Kilroy seemed to possess this skill in spades. Even for vampires, he was quiet.

I woke up the next morning from a glorious slumber alone. No Kilroy to be found. How did he get out of the coffin without making a sound? Or rather, should I be asking how he lulled me into such a deep sleep?

I lifted the coffin lid, but when I peeked out, there was no Kilroy in the hotel room either. He hadn't completely vanished. One of his Hawaiian shirts was draped over the desk chair.

I pushed myself out of the coffin, and when I stood up, a soreness hit my stomach and legs. I had engaged my core all right. Last night's surfing lesson came roaring back into my mind, bringing with it a smile.

I surfed on a volcano.

Despite being undead for centuries, I didn't have a long list of adventures to boast of. I lived a modest afterlife which I was satisfied with. Yet now, I could add surfing.

Adventure accomplished. Time to return to my regularly-scheduled vacation of solitude.

Kilroy left a note on the desk alerting me that he'd gone downstairs for breakfast, but he was saving me a seat. Usually, I skipped breakfast, but it would be rude if I didn't make an exception.

I got dressed with surprising speed, throwing on a fresh shirt and pants. I tried to do that thing where I put my shoes on while standing up thinking it would save me time, but I only succeeded in falling on my ass. I knocked into the desk chair, and a photograph fluttered from the front pocket of Kilroy's discarded shirt.

I had a twinge of envy for fresh vampires. They could easily access pictures of themselves. They could print out photographs and always remember what they looked like. Kilroy posed in a silly picture with what I assumed were his ChoBros. They were of different heights and ethnicities, yet they all looked the same. Same outfits, same sun-kissed skin, same lazy smiles. But Kilroy was by far the best looking. Unlike the pale skin I was used to, his human flesh was bronzed, his hair a golden hue.

Would there have ever been a situation in the human world where our paths crossed? I couldn't imagine my human self traveling to beaches. I liked to think I wasn't dissimilar to how I was now: intellectual, bookish, preferring to acquire knowledge over acquiring a tan. Even in the vampire world, it took a hotel mixup for Kilroy and I to wind up in the same orbit. We were empirically different people.

I quirked an eyebrow when I flipped over the photograph. "Black Fortress" was scrawled across the back. Why did a picture taken on the beach have the name of an Icelandic landmark on the back?

Before I could think on it more, the wall clock struck nine. I rushed out the door to catch the end of breakfast.

It was impossible not to feel a sense of grandeur as you descended the staircase into the lobby. The steps were wide and imposing and looked out over the whole scene, vampires coming and going. I made my way to the bustling hotel restaurant, nestled in a cavernous pocket of the lobby. Every table was full with gregarious travelers loading up on energy before an exciting night. They were all so bright-eyed and chatty. Hence why I usually skipped breakfast.

Kilroy shot his arm up to beckon me. He sat at a round table with two other vampires who shared his youthful spunk. They seemed to be fast friends.

"Hey. Good evening, sleepyhead," he said when I approached. Kilroy drizzled blood-infused syrup over his short stack of pancakes.

(For those disgusted at our meal offerings, keep in mind that for vampires, blood was like butter. It made everything delicious. If Ina Garten were a vampire, you could bet your flesh-and-blood ass that she'd be cooking with gallons of blood.)

"Hello," I replied, then waved at the other guests. "How's breakfast?"

"So good." Kilroy underscored this with a double thumbs up while holding a fork and knife. "I just ate the best bacon I've ever had. I was going to wake you, but you looked so peaceful."

Did that mean Kilroy watched me sleep? A quick flush of heat crept up my neck. For the love of Dracula, two nights with this guy, and he had me acting like a teenager.

"Guys, this is Magnus." Kilroy gestured at me. "He's my roommate. He knows a lot about being a vampire. Magnus, this is Alvin and Simon."

The two vampires did some variation of nodding and waving to acknowledge my presence. Alvin had a long face and wore a baggy hoodie like he quite literally rolled out of a coffin. His friend Simon had at least combed his hair, but wore a tie dye Grateful Dead shirt. He hadn't gotten the memo that the vampire tie dye craze was over.

"Nice to meet all of you. Where's Theodore?" I joked.

"He thought he would be safe looking at the solar eclipse a few years ago," Simon said with a sigh. "We all told him not to chance it..."

"But he chanced it." Alvin rubbed his friend's back. "Spoiler alert: solar eclipses aren't safe for vampires."

"Oh. Sorry." I bowed my head.

"We all just met," Kilroy said and let out an "isn't that wild?" guffaw. "I couldn't find a table for myself, so they invited me to join them. They knew the guy who created *Alvin and the Chipmunks*. He based it on them."

"And then when we got bitten, he claimed he came up with Alvin, Simon, and Theodore all on his own. Laughed his way to the bank." Alvin shook his head. "Putz."

"Anyway, these guys are super cool. And who wants to eat breakfast in silence?" Kilroy asked, getting nods of approval.

I was used to eating in silence. I didn't have to listen to anyone chew.

"Have you guys been to the volcanoes? You can stand on top of one!" Kilroy said excitedly. Alvin and Simon chimed in with their recommendations of the best volcanoes to visit. I stood by the table awkwardly, not sure whether I should sit or not.

Alvin turned to me. His abundant shag of hair fell in his eyes. He was lucky. He was bitten before he started balding. "Is it true you knew Einar when he was a baby?"

"It is. He was an ankle biter, literally. Even since he could sit up, he's loved vampires."

"Far out," Simon said.

"When I see old people, I forget that they used to be babies," Kilroy said, taking a sip of his Mimosa, which in vampire world was champagne mixed with—you guessed it—blood. "Like I know that everyone starts off as a baby and grows up, but some people just look like they were born fifty-five."

Did he cut his eyes to me when he said that? I could've been a rollicking child for all he knew.

"Have you guys gone to the tightrope walk across the two mountains?" Simon asked.

"There's a tightrope walk?" Kilroy's eyes jutted from his head. "That sounds so dope."

"I heard that the views aren't that great," Simon said.

And on they went. They traded thoughts on activities and suggestions for what else to do. Even though they'd only met this morning, they chatted as if they'd known each other for a while. They all had the gift of gab, something I seemed to be born without. No matter how old I was, the feeling of being excluded always felt fresh and raw. So much for Kilroy being shy. Maybe he'd found the right people. Or maybe he only said that to make me feel better. Either way, I didn't want to drag down his vacation.

"I'm not really a breakfast person, so I'm gonna go back to the room and put together my itinerary for the day." I had no itinerary. My vacation was supposed to be filled with alone time. "It was great meeting all of you. I'm sure I'll see you around."

It almost looked like Kilroy's face fell for a second, but I was likely imagining that. I turned and left before he could say anything. I hightailed it to the grand staircase and began the ascent to my room.

Why was I feeling this sharp pang in my chest? Whatever was going on in my head and my chest was one-sided and need not travel past my skeleton.

The room was empty and quiet when I returned. Exactly what I wanted.

I pulled a book from my suitcase. Even with all the time in the world that comes with immortality, my TBR list was still out of control. I plunked myself in the desk chair, kicked my legs onto the desk, and lost myself in a book. This was what vacation was all about. Reading, avoiding social interactions, and having someone make your bed for you.

I only got two pages in when a knock at the window distracted me. Was it a bird that had gotten lost?

No, it was Kilroy.

Kilroy?!

He stood on the narrow ledge giving me a casual wave. I responded by nearly leaping out of my skin and then falling out of my chair.

14

KILROY

Major vampire plus: We had the ability to leap up to window ledges. Why did I even bother turning into a bat when I could just pogo stick my way here and there?

"Kilroy!" Magnus yelled through the glass.

I maintained a straight face. It wasn't nice to laugh at people who fell out of chairs.

"What the hell are you doing out there?" Magnus said once he opened the window.

"Just hangin' out." I shrugged my shoulders, playing it cool even though the wind was being a pain in my undead ass.

"We need to get you inside! You could fall!"

I couldn't help but smile at the panic in his voice. For a man who came off as refined and collected, it was a kick watching him freak out. I didn't want to scare him too much, though. I came inside without a fight and dusted off the snow that had accumulated on my shoulders.

"What are you doing?"

"We can leap to great heights. Might as well take advantage of it to prank my roommate." I sat on the coffin lid. "What are you up to?"

I pulled a piece of bacon from the front pocket of my Hawaiian shirt and snapped off a piece.

"I'm reading." Magnus showed off an open book for proof.

"You bailed on breakfast to read a book?"

"I didn't bail. I'm not really a breakfast eater."

"Yeah, it's weird to eat breakfast when it's dark out, but food is food." I gobbled up the rest of my bacon strip. I was relieved to discover that vampires still liked bacon.

"You know your shirt is going to smell like bacon for the rest of the day."

"Yeah. Isn't it awesome? If I'm ever feeling down..." I sniffed my pocket. "Ahhhh."

A smile fought through on Magnus's lips. Watching him try not to enjoy himself was almost as fun as watching him enjoy himself.

"You should've stayed. Those guys are cool. Maybe we can all hang out."

"Lovely. You'll have fun."

I sensed a cold front that rivaled the weather outside. Did Magnus wake up on the wrong side of the coffin?

"You will, too. It would've been cool if you stayed, even though you're not a breakfast guy."

"I didn't want to disturb you and your friends."

"They're not my friends. I mean, they're not not my friends. We only just met. They're nice. Simon was bit at Woodstock. He was so high, it took him two hours to realize he'd been turned into a vampire."

"What a story," he deadpanned. I detected an edge to his voice. He sat back down and returned to his book.

"Hold up." I pushed the book down, forcing him to look at me. "What's going on?"

"Nothing. I don't want to disturb your schedule. Alvin and Simon seem fun. I get why you'd want to spend your vacation with them."

"Uh, who said that?"

Magnus looked up at me. Did he think I was ditching him?

"Is this all you have planned today? Reading?" I wasn't against reading by any means, but his book was getting on my nerves.

"Yes. That is what I would like to do on my vacation."

"No. You want to mope." I removed his book from his hands and placed it on the desk. "Yes, being a vampire can be lonely. And yes, being a vampire can be a drag. But so can being a human. Have you ever had to stand in line at the DMV?"

"I'm not sure what that is."

"Consider yourself lucky. Very lucky." I sat on the desk, giving him no choice but to make eye contact. I remembered all over again how opaque his eyes were, two fierce gray orbs.

"What are you proposing then?"

"We are in a beautiful country and have nearly an entire day of darkness. Just because we're immortal doesn't mean we should let days like this go to waste. And even though you've been a vampire for like ever, there's still some cool stuff you haven't done yet. You haven't fully taken advantage of all your powers, and I want to show you how awesome being a vampire is."

I wondered how long it'd been since he had an all-out fun day. He'd probably spent years mourning Gunnar and trudging through life. Magnus deserved to have a let loose.

"Are you sure? I don't want you to spend your whole vacation entertaining me. You came here to have fun."

"Entertaining you is fun." I looked down and found my hand atop his. No big deal, right?

"Okay." He pushed back from the desk and stood up, putting his lips parallel to mine.

Not like I was thinking of that.

"I suppose I can take one day and make it more outdoors-focused."

"That's the spirit!" I hopped off the desk and headed to the door.

"Kilroy, are you sure you don't want to change out of your beach outfit?"

I looked down at my Hawaiian shirt and shorts. The cold didn't bother me, and more importantly, I looked rad as hell.

"Nah."

I opened the door, and we exited into the hall.

"So what's first?"

A mischievous grin took over my lips. "Now Magnus, do you really think I'd ruin the surprise? Where's the fun in that?"

15

MAGNUS

"I've been sledding," I told Kilroy.

The first stop on this secret itinerary took us to the top of a ski slope. A vast white wilderness dotted with thick evergreen trees greeted us. It made me feel like a speck upon this giant earth.

The sled hung from Kilroy's hands. It was a classic wooden model with red metal runners underneath. My guess was that he borrowed it from Einar, and it was custom made over a hundred years ago. The quality was impeccable. But again, this wasn't my first sledding rodeo.

Kilroy dropped the sled at his feet.

"You've been sledding, but you've never been Extreme Vampire Sledding." He threw out his arms and wiggled his fingers in a ta-da flourish.

"Is Extreme Vampire Sledding real?" I knew that extreme sports were popular among young, male humans. Did Kilroy attend mixed martial arts competitions in his past life?

"It is starting today." He wrapped an arm around my back as we gazed out on the snowy landscape. "Normal human sledding would have you go down a small hill. But we're going to take it one step further. We're going down this mountainside in a sled."

"Sledding is best when you do it on a hill without obstructions." Our mountainside had clusters of trees.

"Maybe if you're a mere mortal. But we are not. We are going to bob and weave our way down this mountain, using our heightened senses to dodge trees and rocks. There's going to be sharp, hairpin turns. Mother Nature is going to be the raggedy-ass bitch she is and throw everything in our way."

"We could sail right into a tree."

"And?"

"And…" Not die. We might sustain some injuries, but vampires had stronger bodies that could withstand more than the average human.

"At most, we'll have battle scars."

"We're going to take this mountain in just a sled?" The reality of the situation hit me, how impossible and blatantly crazy this seemed. Kilroy was loving it.

"I haven't even mentioned the best part."

"What?" I steeled myself.

"We're doing it blindfolded." He pulled two black blindfolds from his pocket.

"Where did you get those?"

"Einar always keeps a box of them at the front desk for guests. Vampires are into some kinky shit. No judgment here."

He twirled his finger, signaling me to turn around. I could put on a blindfold by myself, but he seemed insistent to do it himself. Why stand in his way?

My world went black as the satin strip of fabric covered my eyes. My heart began to race. Whatever the vampire's version of pulse was pounding in my ears. There was very little medical research out there on how vampire bodies worked, so we just had to roll with things.

"Nervous?" he asked, right in my ear, sending a deep shiver down my spine.

"Yes," I said. But I wasn't sure what I was more nervous about: sledding down a mountainside or being blindfolded for Kilroy.

He took my hand and led me to sit on the sled. I straddled the seat, practically folding my body to fit. Kilroy sat down behind me, the faint smell of sandalwood filling my nose. Like in the coffin, he was flush against me and pulled me close to him. It was natural at this point.

"You ready?" he asked, his deep voice taking up rent in my ear.

The sled inched forward, crunching slowly through the snow. I could feel gravity wanting to pull us down the mountain.

"Let's do it." I gave us the final nudge forward.

The sled dragged for a moment, not really going anywhere, like a crawl through a traffic jam. I thought about giving it another nudge, until physics, and a little bit of magic, took hold.

The sled dipped downward, and then we were flying.

Wind whipped through my hair and blasted against my face. I was on the tip of a rocket ship, hurtling through space and time and leaving the normal rules of earth behind. Snow fluttered against my eyelashes and whizzed by my ears. I responded by letting out a laugh that was as much a scream.

"You okay?" Kilroy yelled.

"Woohoo!" I was on top of the world. Not being able to see meant I could hear, smell, taste and feel with greater power. That plus my existing enhanced senses meant I was reaching a new plane of existence. I had extra-heightened senses of everything going on around me: The exact sound of the sled slicing through the snow. The unique smell and taste of cold wind. And the touch of Kilroy's strong hands wrapped around me.

Every fiber of me coursed with crackling energy. I might've been dead, but I'd never felt more alive.

"Turn to the right!" Kilroy yelled.

I sensed it, too. The pine tree we were headed for. The smell of pine hit my nose for a second before I had to pull the reins and turn us left. I had no idea we had this kind of sensory power.

"Right!" he yelled. I was already on top of it. The crackle of a pinecone crinkling under the sled filled my ears. We continued to slalom through the trees, riding the waves of snow under our feet. I engaged my core to keep steady, pulling the invisible string from my belly button to my spine.

I steered us with precision that could have landed us on the Olympic bobsled team—if they accepted vampires.

Kilroy's lips rested on my shoulder, and while I wondered if he was kissing me, I crashed us into a snowbank. We blew through the wall of snow, sending cold dust sprinkling over my cheeks, and came to a stop.

I came back down to earth, literally and figuratively, as we reached the base of the mountain.

Kilroy untied my blindfold, and when the fabric fell from my eyes, his big, goofy, snow-shellacked smile greeted me.

"What'd you think?" he asked. We were both catching our breaths.

"That was…a dangerous daredevil stunt. And I loved it."

He gave me two thumbs up, and I returned the gesture. Two thumbs way up.

"See, toldja there's cool stuff to do as a vampire." He flopped into the snow and made a snow angel. "Isn't it awesome that I can do this without a coat? I don't have to worry about frostbite!"

Kilroy's mind switched to different ideas faster than our sled bobbed between trees. When he was done, I pulled him up so he didn't ruin his perfect angel.

"Whoa." He stared at his creation in wonder.

"It's a snow angel. Millions of children do these every winter."

"I didn't know if we'd be able to since it's an angel."

"Well, we're not demons, so it's okay."

16

KILROY

We took the long way through the woods en route back to the hotel to enjoy the quiet and vastness of the winter landscape. Why did I ever shit on winter so much? It was as gorgeous as a beach. Huge pine trees and expansive cliffs surrounded us. These were views only the most fearless human explorers could reach, but for two vampires, it could be a simple hiking trail.

Magnus walked ahead of me. He broke off two thick branches from a nearby tree and used them as walking sticks. I checked out his ass, because that was a thing I did now. Alvin and Simon told me they were friends who dated women as humans, but as vampires, they started hooking up. It wasn't as if we had to worry about the social stigmas. Vampires seemed to have a live and let live policy. We had enough to worry about with stakers and staying out of the sun. Might as well enjoy eternity.

So I continued to check out Magnus's ass as he bent over. And maybe imagined putting my tongue in it. Because that could also be a thing I did now.

This guy was taking over my vacation and my mind.

"Did you know vampires can grab snow with our bare hands?" Magnus spun around and nailed me with a snowball to the chest.

"I believe that was a direct hit." He flashed me a victorious grin.

"Nice aim!" I brushed the remaining snowball off my chest, which left my shirt wet and clinging to my chest. I thought I caught Magnus checking me out, but he was already squatting down, making another snowball.

"And with our enhanced strength, we can make extra-large snowballs." He rapidly amassed a mammoth ball the size of a bowling ball. He heaved it over his head and propelled it straight at me.

Shit. The time for lingering glances was over. It was war.

I leapt out of the way just in time. Snow exploded behind me as I crawled behind a snow bank. I set out to build a war chest of snowballs. Magnus was right: My hands worked double-time, faster than I'd ever seen them work as a human, gobbling together snowballs.

"Kilroy?" he called out.

I lobbed a snowball with ferocious velocity. It smacked him square between the eyes. Score!

Magnus shook it off Terminator-style and kept going, hurling another bowling snowball at my head.

"You gotta up your game, Magnus, because vampires can quickly jump out of the way," I said, leaping to the top branch of a tree. "And we have the power of sneak attacks."

I threw two more snowballs at him. I took a half-second to admire the view of the forest, a view no human had ever experienced.

When I looked down again, Magnus was gone. The ground was eerily peaceful.

"Uh, Magnus? Where'd you go?"

The impact of a snowball clouded my vision. I wiped away the white dust. Magnus gave me two trolling thumbs up from the top of a neighboring tree. A wicked, almost childlike sense of glee took over his face.

I jumped to another tree, then another. I closed my eyes and listened for the rustling of Magnus's movement. Not seeing him but sensing him, I arced my arm back and let go a line drive of a snowball. It slammed into his shoulder, but not before he hurled one that barreled into my chest.

"You're not the only vampire with enhanced hearing to find his enemies." Magnus juggled four snowballs while balancing on the point of a mighty pine tree.

"How am I just finding out you can juggle?"

"I have a lot of time on my hands."

"Circus freak!" I yelled back.

We devolved into a full-blown snowball fight, throwing and dodging with supernatural aplomb. We hopped through the trees trying to catch each other. My lungs filled with joyous air. I hadn't felt this free, this wild since my surfing days, when the ocean felt like one giant playground.

My grumpy roommate was gone, replaced with this maniacally happy vampire. I was just hoping to show Magnus a good time. I didn't expect him to be as ecstatic as a kid hopped up on sugar at his birthday party.

We chased each other through the forest. Our snowballs were like cannonballs, large and forceful. Every time one of his projectiles hit me, it was like another shock from a defibrillator waking me up.

"Did you just throw a snowball at my ass?" I asked after a direct hit.

"Maybe."

"You're dead, Magnus!"

"The joke's on you. I'm already dead."

He chased me through a thicket of trees. I ran and laughed at the same time, my lungs confused at what to do. I came out the other side to a cliff that overlooked an expansive valley. There was no place else to run. Magnus charged at me, not yet realizing that our options were limited.

We barreled off the cliff, tumbling down the side, becoming two snowballs ourselves. Magnus landed on top of me when we reached the bottom. His wide gray eyes sparkled inches from my face, glinting in the moonlight, a sign of life in this pale wilderness. I pushed back a lock of his perfectly combed hair that fell in his face, letting my fingers graze his clean-shaven cheek.

He licked his red lips, not taking his gaze off me. Heat built between us, enough to melt this mountain range into the ocean.

We were close. Desperately close. I wanted to kiss him so badly, feel his breath in my chest, taste his tongue in my mouth.

But whatever moment I was imagining faded away, a summer rainstorm that was torrential downpour one minute and clear skies the next.

Magnus sat up, wiped snow from his shoulders. The gleeful expression was put away, and his normal reserved grin returned as he stared at something behind me.

"What is it?" I asked.

He pointed, his expression getting more ominous. I sat up and followed his gaze to a human campsite set up a few feet away.

17

KILROY

I shuffled out from under him and brushed off the snow clinging to my clothes.

A bright blue tent sat in the middle of a circle of trees. It glowed from the inside thanks to a lantern that was still on. The remnants of a fire was close by.

I tensed with fear. My stomach had no such reservations. It rumbled with a ravenous hunger.

Magnus pulled me behind a tree. He peeked at the campsite.

"Is it weird that I'm scared and hungry?" I asked.

"It's because you smell blood."

I was like a kid on Thanksgiving possessed by the smells of fresh-cooked food coming from the kitchen but forced to wait hours until we could eat.

"We should go," Magnus said. He kept a protective hand on my hip, keeping me behind the tree.

"Wait." I was impulsive, though, and I shoved forward to catch a glimpse. "There's no movement coming from the tent."

"They could be out on a hunt."

"Then why would they leave their lantern on? Wouldn't they want to conserve energy since they're in the middle of nowhere?"

While Magnus chewed on that new piece to the puzzle, I tested my hypothesis by throwing a small rock at the tent. It bounced off the side and flopped into the snow.

"Kilroy, stop!" Magnus whisper-yelled at me.

I wasn't as scared as him because I knew we could turn into bats in a matter of seconds.

"Look." I pointed at the tent. "Nobody reacted."

The lantern created a silhouette effect turning the objects inside into shadow puppets. The shadow puppets didn't budge.

"Isn't it typical to have a person stay behind as lookout or something? That's what my ChoBros and I did when we camped on the beach to make sure animals didn't come."

Magnus tapped his fingers on the tree in deliberation. I already had my answer, though.

I walked to the tent.

"Kilroy!" Magnus whisper-yelled behind me.

"Hello! Humans!" I called into the tent. "Did anybody order a large pizza with pepperoni and banana peppers?"

No answer. No stirring. I walked around the perimeter to get a better look at the silhouettes.

"Anybody home?"

The tent had an eerie silence as if it were a haunted house, and I was the dumb comic relief who had to check it out.

I shrugged to Magnus, who remained behind the tree. I unzipped the tent and had my suspicions confirmed.

The dead bodies of two explorers lay in sleeping bags side-by-side, with a lantern glowing between them. I checked each of their pulses to confirm they had passed on.

I poked my head from the tent and gave Magnus a thumbs-up to join. I ran my thumb across my throat so he knew what was up.

"How long have they been dead?" I asked Magnus once he arrived in the tent.

"I'd say less than a day. Maybe just a few hours. Their bodies aren't frozen yet." I leaned down to get a better look at them. They were about my age and in good shape. Any human who dared travel up here had to be in tiptop form to survive as long as they did.

"What were they doing up here?" I wondered aloud.

"They came here to kill us." Magnus handed over a book he found in the corner. *So You Wanna Slay Vampires?*

"Hmm. I won't be adding that one to my TBR list."

I pulled back the sleeping bag of the male explorer. Clutched in his hand was a sharp stake. The sight of it made me stumble back, a sharp pang of fear hitting my chest. It was one thing to hear about slayers, but quite another to see their crude weapons solely meant to stab someone like me.

I opened their duffel bag and found a cache of stakes.

"Damn. These people meant business." I scratched my back with a stake.

"Careful!" Magnus smacked it out of my hand. He shut the duffel bag so roughly the zipper almost broke.

I studied the male explorer. He looked no different than the guys I saw out on the surf. We could've been friends, even ChoBros, in the human world.

"Listen to this." Magnus read from a journal that was under their lamp. "'December 26th. Each day, we are making more progress to the top of the mountain where the supposed vampire lair is. We are one step closer to fulfilling our destiny of cleansing God's beautiful earth of these disgusting, immoral creatures. Also, I wish I'd packed more

Oreos. I ate through my secret stash in one day.'" Magnus rolled his eyes. "Magellan, he is not."

"That's what slayers think of us?" I asked.

"That's what all humans think of us." Magnus tossed the journal onto the explorer, and it smacked him in the face.

"If God didn't want there to be vampires, then why did he create vampires? That's on him," I said. We were part of God's plan. We had to be. I wasn't sure how exactly we fit into the ecosystem, but I was certain there were blueprints. "I'm not disgusting or immoral. They don't even know me. I'm nice! I can't help it that I'm a vampire. I was killed this way."

Magnus felt their necks. "They haven't completely frozen over. They're still warm."

"They're just going to go to waste out here." My stomach rumbled. "What happens if we bite a dead person? Do they become a vampire?"

"No. We can only turn living humans into vampires."

"So technically, we aren't breaking your moral code."

"Correct. Additionally, they are so far from a human encampment that there's a good chance a search party wouldn't find them. I'm amazed they made us this far north. They're likely presumed dead."

"And if we left these people, then we would be letting perfectly good blood go to waste. Think of all the starving vampires in the world." I licked my lips. My stomach rumbled with insatiable hunger.

"We have to do it for the starving vampires."

"Exactly."

Magnus clapped his hands together. "All right. That's enough justification."

"Thank goodness. Let's dig in!"

18

MAGNUS

After our glorious feast, we stumbled back to the hotel. It was a struggle, each step feeling more leaden than the previous one. We were in a food coma. Kilroy wanted to sleep it off in the tent, but for some reason, that seemed to cross a line. Sure, we could feast on their corpses, but that didn't mean we had a right to use their property. We weren't Goldilocks. She was quite rude.

I exhaled a sigh of relief when we reached the lobby. It was an oasis of warmth and light. Crackling fireplaces and warm candlelight adorned the massive space making it feel cozy.

"I am going to take the longest nap." Kilroy collapsed on the nearest couch.

"Not here." I kicked his legs off. "This is the lobby."

"Then why are these couches so comfortable?" Kilroy sunk into the cushions, really playing it up.

"You can take a nap upstairs."

"Should we try and hold out? When is the sun coming up?"

"We have time." Thank goodness for Iceland's interminable darkness. "We can take a nap and go out later tonight."

Kilroy's eyes were closed, yet he still quirked a shit-eating eyebrow.

"What?" I asked.

"You want to go out tonight? I thought you wanted to spend this vacation holed up in your room."

"It's a figure of speech." Yet I was surprised I said it. I was an indoor vampire, but tonight had been a marathon of extreme outdoors activity. And it was fun! "Let's just go upstairs."

Kilroy peeled himself off the couch, as if a giant magnet was pulling him. I had to keep him steady until he reached the stairs. That man could not hold his blood.

"I'll meet you up there. I just have to check on something with the front desk," I said.

Kilroy gave a flimsy wave and continued his drunken march up the grand staircase. I watched him go. He went to say hello to a pair of vampires coming downstairs, but a burp came out instead.

"Sorry. My bad," he uttered and continued in silence.

Once he was out of sight, I made my way to the front desk and tapped the bell for service. Einar appeared, smiling but weary. Did the man ever sleep?

"Magnus, how is everything working out?"

"Fine," I said in an understatement. "Kilroy and I are making it work."

"Wonderful. Thank you again for being understanding and accommodating."

"Of course." I leaned in, ensuring no one else was in ear shot. "I was wondering if you could help me with something."

"Yes. Anything."

"I need your help to reserve a space in town for later this evening. There are some other items I'll need your help setting up. Or Reynar's, since he's more technologically savvy. Would you be amenable to assisting me with this request?"

"Certainly. What is it for?"

"I have an idea for an evening activity for myself and Kilroy, but it will require some coordination."

"Like a date?" Einar's bushy eyebrow moved north on his wrinkled forehead.

"What? No. Not a date. It's an evening activity."

"For you and Mr. Kilroy…"

"Precisely." Perhaps the man was getting a bit too long in the tooth since he was having trouble understanding.

"In my world, we call that a date."

"In your world, people have to use elevators."

Einar continued looking at me and smiling, every crease on his face coming to life at my expense. Heat rose in my neck, as if he'd thrown me into a boiling cauldron.

"Einar, it's not what you're thinking. Get those presumptions out of your head. Kilroy is my roommate. We've managed to turn an awkward situation into a burgeoning friendship. That is all. Stop looking at me like that."

"Whatever you say, Magnus."

"So you'll be able to help me?"

"As you wish."

I strummed my fingers on the counter. "And could you possibly get us a reservation at one of the speakeasies in town?"

"My pleasure. Because every evening activity should include a candlelight dinner, too."

I scoffed. I was being trolled by a ninety-year-old human. How humiliating.

"I meant a *friendly* candlelight dinner." He chuckled to himself as he jotted down notes on his pad.

"Why are you acting like this? I thought we were friends."

"Because in all the years of you coming here, this is the first time you asked me to plan a special evening for you and another person."

"I had lots of special evenings with Gunnar."

"Which he planned."

Gunnar was both the more spontaneous one and the planner in our relationship. I was perpetually in favor of staying home.

"Just because I want to plan an activity doesn't mean anything, Einar."

"And you're blushing."

"Am not." I would kill to be able to use a mirror right now. Well, not literally kill. Figure of speech.

Einar picked up the phone and gave the "one minute" finger gesture. "Reynar, can you swing by the front desk to help with something."

"Thank you for roping Reynar in. He can probably help with my request and will be a professional whilst doing so."

Reynar marched up to the desk a moment later with a box of candles under his arm. I wanted to believe the mystique that they handmade all the candles in the lobby, but the reality was more mundane.

"Hello, Mr. Magnus. Grandfather, what do you need?"

"Help me out with something," Einar said. "Magnus is blushing right now, isn't he?"

"Einar!" I gasped out.

Reynar turned to give me a look, but it only took him a second to make his decision. "Oh, yeah. Totally. One hundred percent."

"I am going to figure out how to use the internet, then I'm going to post a negative review of this establishment. Beautiful aesthetic. Nosy innkeepers."

Einar and Reynar high-fived.

19

KILROY

When I got back to the room, I passed out. I was wiped from today, and that, uh, afternoon snack was incredibly filling.

I didn't know how long I'd been asleep when the coffin lid creaked open. I peeked my eyes open.

"Morning? Afternoon? Evening?" I asked.

"Evening."

"Evening, Magnus!" I stretched my arms to the ceiling letting out a ferocious yawn. Why was it that napping only made me more tired?

"Were you able to nap?"

"Heck yes. Do you ever dream about your human life?" I had a dream where me and Robert Downey Jr. were eating cheeseburgers in my elementary school library. Like all of my dreams, I had no idea what it meant.

"I probably did at one point, but those memories eventually fade away." Magnus shrugged nonchalantly. His human life was beyond the rearview mirror.

I checked the clock on the wall. It was the wee hours of the morning.

"What should we do with the rest of our night? Did you want to go downstairs and grab dinner? Or you know what? You probably want to chill on your own."

A smile perked on his lips. "Actually, I have our evening mapped out. Get dressed. We're going out."

Magnus and I headed into town, which had been blanketed with a fresh layer of snow undisturbed by humans. It was three in the morning for them. They were sound asleep.

I decided to get dressed up for the occasion, whatever it might be. Magnus was always well-dressed. It wouldn't hurt if I followed suit. Well, not an actual suit. I wore a sweater and khakis, which was as formal as I got in my human life. Surfers had no need for three-piece suits.

"So where are we going?" I asked for the third time since we left the hotel.

"I told you. It's a surprise. The point of a surprise is not to give away the surprise before it's time."

"That's cool. That's cool." I sidled up to Magnus. "Can I get a hint?"

"No."

"I'm going to use reverse psychology and guess that no is actually a secret hint."

"That's not reverse psychology."

"And how would you know?" I nudged my elbow against his arm.

"Because I've read nearly every book on the subject."

"Whoa."

"I've had time on my hands. I could've gotten a PhD in psychology and several other subjects, but I didn't feel like sitting in a classroom. That, and I didn't want to take on student loans. Even in death, they couldn't be discharged."

I liked to think skipping college to chase the surf was the smartest thing I'd done with my life.

We walked down the middle of the street. Lights were strung in a zigzag pattern above us. It was objectively romantic, if one were looking for romance.

"You're taking me into town because there's a cool store you want me to see. Oh, or there's a sculpture I should check out."

"Incorrect on both counts."

"I got it. We're going to scare humans. We'll jump up to their windows and stare at them while they sleep. And then when they wake up, we'll go 'I vant to zuck your blood. Muahaha!'"

"No vampire talks like that."

"Tell that to humans."

"One vampire spoke in that accent centuries ago, and now the human population thinks we all have that dialect." Magnus laughed to himself. Where was Magnus from? Did he even remember? He sounded refined, like he was either from England or grew up really rich. Or hell, he could've been from the middle of Ohio for all I knew.

Wherever he came from, his deep, confident voice was doing something to me, making those funny feelings in my stomach get stronger. It wasn't just my newfound bisexual lust that he was stirring.

"Kilroy, I'm sorry to inform you that you haven't been close at all. I recommend you not audition for a game show because your guessing skills aren't up to par. As surfers like to say, 'ride the wave.'" He threw an arm around me, delivering more funny feelings.

"That's my line."

We continued walking down the main drag. Twinkling lights spun around lampposts and around front windows. It was all impossibly charming. What was this town like during the day? Was it full of touristy shoppers or locals?

Were there musicians who played on the corner? It hit me that I would never know.

We turned down a narrow, dark cobblestone road. Our hands dangled close to each other.

"Here we are."

The bright lights of a marquee shined in the darkness, the one sign of life on the street. The name of the old theater twinkled above in blinking lights. It beckoned us like a lighthouse. A box office booth stood in the center of the entrance.

"We're seeing a movie?" I asked.

"When I first started coming to the hotel, this theater played silent films. A pianist would sit at the front and play over the film. Then talkies came. Then blockbusters. And now..." The coming soon posters hanging on the wall were sequels and reboots to films from a decade ago. "Dreck."

I threw my head back to take in the scope of the marquee. "It's beautiful."

Inside, the theater was full of old charm. It resisted the urge to remodel and modernize. We walked through a grand lobby with red carpeting and posters of old films aglow with light bulbs around the perimeter.

The buttery smell of popcorn filled the theater lobby. There was something about the scent of movie theater popcorn that was unique and timeless. I squatted down to check out the candy available at concessions.

"What's your favorite candy?" I asked. "It's Red Vines for me. Do vampires eat candy at the movies?"

"Sometimes this theater will play special vampire-only screenings overnight and put out vampire-centric concessions."

I skimmed my fingers across the glass. Memories of

going to the movies as a kid popped in my head. "My dad would get a tub of popcorn and dump Raisinets in, then mix them together."

"Sounds sticky."

"It was," I said with nostalgic delight.

"I prefer pretzel bites with a side of cheese, although I highly doubt that's actual cheese."

I snorted. "What's the vampire version of Red Vines?"

"Human veins."

Upstairs, Magnus had us sit in the front bow of the balcony. A red curtain covered the screen.

"So what movie are we seeing?"

"It's a surprise."

"Can I get a hint? Can we do charades?"

Magnus patted me on the knee and added a soft rub. "Trust me. You'll want to be surprised."

He turned around and signaled to the projectionist. The lights went down.

My anticipation hit a fever pitch. What kind of movie did Magnus think I would enjoy? Would it be a comedy or an action film or maybe a scary movie with vampires?

The curtain parted and a second later, we were on a sunny beach in Hawaii. A few seconds after that, we were riding a massive wave, one that took up the whole, gigantic screen. We were sliding through the tail pipe as the water curled around us.

I was instantly hurtled back to sunny shores. Memories flooded my mind. I could taste the salty water, feel the sand between my toes, and hear the waves crash. The film cut to a sunrise in New Zealand, the sky filling with brushstrokes of oranges and pinks before the sun peeked over the horizon.

It was majestic and more beautiful than I remembered. I

hadn't seen the sun in months. I felt myself starting to forget what shade of blue the sky was. Until now.

"What do you think?" Magnus asked.

I couldn't respond. All I could do was let the tears fall from my eyes.

20

MAGNUS

Reynar had helped me find a surfing documentary we could screen. It followed a group of surfers taking on the most dangerous and gorgeous waves in the world. Shot after shot was of sunny locales and surfers flying on the tip of tides and perfect beach sunsets that sparkled on the whitecaps. The sounds of crashing waves, ocean breezes, and cawing seagulls poured through the surround sound.

When I looked over, Kilroy was crying.

I could only imagine what he was thinking, what he was feeling. I started to panic. Was this film making him upset? Was it making him miss the human world too much?

Kilroy's hand squeezed mine on our shared armrest. I looked over, and he smiled at me through his tears. Were those sad or happy tears? Maybe both, the kind of tears that savored what you had while knowing you'd never have it again.

"Thank you," he said, his voice catching in his throat. He squeezed my hand harder. An emotional Kilroy was new, but it only made my heart swell for him more.

He was fully invested in the movie, adding in commentary in parts. He guffawed at wipeouts, nodded his head at confessionals, and provided his opinion of surf technique. Surfing was more difficult than I suspected. He was an expert. Listening to him was like hearing a lecture from an academic.

One of the final surfs had the guys in South America hitting the waves as the sun set in front of them. It was a huge, mighty sun, flaming all kinds of reds before the film faded to black. It took my breath away.

I turned to Kilroy, who remained staring at the black screen.

"Did you enjoy that? If you ever find yourself missing the sun and the beach, you can return to this film. Or others. There are a multitude of documentaries on surfing, to my surprise."

I was rambling, waiting for Kilroy to interject. Quiet Kilroy was unnerving.

He leaned over. I got closer to hear what he was going to say.

Yet there were no words, only a soft kiss planted on my lips. He moved back slowly, his eyes wide and full of vulnerability. We stared at each other intensely, almost like a game of chicken.

I kissed him back. Once our lips collided, our mutual hesitation vanished, replaced with hunger. My chest rattled with delight, with feelings that I didn't know I could still feel. His warm, salty breath sent tingles tumbling down my throat. Kilroy let out the cutest little sound, like a runt.

I ran my fingers through his luscious blond shag, then traced down his neck, feeling him pulsing under my touch.

"This is the nicest thing someone's ever done for me," he said. "I'll never forget this."

"Unfortunately, you will."

He shook his head and stretched his thin lips into a knowing smile. "No, I won't."

Kilroy jumped out of his seat and straddled my legs. My poor seat squeaked under the added weight, the solid craftsmanship no match for a solid man.

"So like, when I was a human, I was only with chicks."

"And now as a vampire, you find yourself lusting after men and women?"

"Yeah. And it doesn't feel weird."

"That feeling of taboo only exists in the human world. Here, we are free."

"You're so smart, Magnus. Just let me know if I'm doing bisexual wrong."

He ground his crotch against mine, our cocks hard and wanting. Nope, he was doing it right.

I clapped my hands on his ass and pulled him to me, our rocking quickly turning into dry thrusts.

Par for the course with vampires. Our bodies were cold, but our sex was hot.

I managed to pull myself away, gasping for air in the process. I stared into his blown-out pupils.

"For the sake of management and the theater's janitorial staff, we should probably pause and pick this back up in our room."

"I thought we had dinner reservations after this." Kilroy kissed down my neck.

Shit.

"We do. You're right."

Kilroy unbuttoned the top button of my shirt. "I could skip dinner."

My cock rutted against his ass. "On second thought, I could, too."

21

MAGNUS

The thing about vampires was that we fucked hard. Maybe it was all the blood in our system, or the shackles of human society freeing our inhibitions. Or perhaps it was the fact that we were alive forever, so we had to work harder to feel pleasure.

Whatever it was, vampires fucked hard. When two people come together who have enhanced strength and are horny?

Watch out.

As soon as I clicked open the door, Kilroy threw me across our hotel room, my body flying in a whoosh before slamming against the wall. He met me before I fell and drugged me with a ferocious kiss that I could feel at the base of my throat.

His heavy-lidded eyes were all pupils, full of life and lust.

"Magnus," he said through moans.

I scrawled my desperate fingers through his locks, pulling him closer to me, our tongues dueling in the liminal space between our mouths. He pressed his tongue against my teeth, forcing them open. A deep groan charged out of me as he swept through my mouth, his hungry breaths filling the silence.

"I want you so bad," he said.

"As do I."

"I love how formal you are." Kilroy dragged his teeth down my neck, pressing into my jugular. "Can vampires bite each other?"

"Only if you want to leave a hickey."

"I'll save that for your inner thigh."

I shivered with anticipation at Kilroy marking my most delicate areas. Lust built up in me, a gushing river no match for the pitiful dam. I yanked off his sweater and undershirt and tossed them to the furthest reaches of this room.

I did what I'd been dying to do for days: ran my hands down his chest, savoring the curve of every muscle, the faint dust of hair below his belly button, the downward slope of his hip muscles leading me to…

"Fuck!" Kilroy threw his head back as I grabbed his bulge. I kept going, because I was a ravenous, greedy mothersucker, slipping my hand into his pants and letting it drift further south. I hummed over the sensitive skin that led to his hot, pulsing hole. I gave it a tap, holding my finger there. Kilroy was all mine. I controlled this strong, confident man with one finger. He lifted his leg, providing further access. I massaged the tight skin. His lips were red and swollen, drenched in desire as he struggled to hold my gaze.

He cracked out a sound that was full of the best kind of agony.

"Yes," he whispered.

"Make no mistake, Kilroy. I am going to devour you tonight."

A smile managed to return to his face. "You know what they say. When the coffin's a rockin', don't come a knockin'."

I pulled back just before breaching his opening. Our tongues tangled in electric heat. He undid my belt and fly. Off went my pants. He shamelessly bit his lip as he glanced downward.

I was rock hard, no longer trying to hide anything. I could sense in his eyes how bad he wanted it.

I hurled him against the coffin.

He winced in pain. Actual pain. I worried for a moment that I'd gone too far before finding relief in his smile.

"Is it just me, or are you super horny?" he asked.

"It's both of us. Vampires are rigorous fornicators."

"Being a vampire is giving me life."

"That's quite literally impossible," I said.

He beckoned me with the curl of a finger. "Get over here, old man."

Old? His wicked smile sent a fresh surge of juice to my loins. *I'll show you old.*

In a flash, I was at his side, picking him up, slamming him onto the desk and kissing down his neck. Hotel stationery fluttered around us in a tornado of paper.

"You're going to break this antique piece of furniture."

"It's not an antique. It's only 200 years old, I'd say. And all the furniture in this room is bolted down."

"Why?"

This time, I was the one with the wicked smile.

"Because of rigorous fornication?" he asked.

"Vampires fuck hard."

As ferocious as we'd be tonight, there were likely past guests who truly tested the limits of the bolts holding the furniture in place.

I kissed him quiet. Kilroy ripped open my shirt, buttons spilling everywhere, tingling on the floor.

"Fuuuuuck yes." He rubbed his hands on my chest, his fingers threading in my chest hair. "I am so ready to get railed."

He got on his knees and took me in his mouth before I could say anything. My verbal abilities were reduced to moans. He disappeared my entire cock in his warm mouth while looking up at me with a fiery gaze. Heat bolted from my balls up my spine. For a first-time cocksucker, he was quite excellent. I was in danger of finishing, but not before the main event.

"You're very good at that," I said.

"Beginner's luck," he answered while slapping my cock on his tongue. He stood up, his lips nice and pink.

I was about to throw him against the coffin again, but in a rush of movement, he propelled us onto the ceiling, the curtains flying up from the residual gust of wind. We hung by the metal rods. I was dizzy from my blood not knowing which head to rush to.

I pushed the light fixture out of our way to kiss.

"Can we have sex on the ceiling?" he asked.

"It requires lots of balance work."

"Good thing we practiced on the volcano." He flexed his abs, shining in the haze of light.

I pulled him flush against me, our cocks poking each other's legs. I slid my finger down his crack and tapped at his hole.

He pushed his pants up, and I helped take them off. Doing this upside down was a two-person job. His cock was thick and pulsing.

I spun myself right-side up and hung by the rod, perfect position to take his cock in my mouth, and for him to do the same. He fucked into my mouth in hard jabs, the taste of bitter pre-come hitting my tongue.

"Watch out for the fangs," he said.

"I know, I know."

"Just saying. Have vampires ever accidentally bitten..."

"It's likely possible but let's not dwell on it." There were billions of vampires in history, and we were cursed with long fangs. There was a vampire who made a killing, no pun intended, selling soft caps to put on fangs. Allegedly, it was for socializing with humans, but the bulk of his consumer base was buying them to have safe sex.

Kilroy let out the most beautiful moans, lilting and almost songlike. I matched him with my deep-throated sounds of pleasure as his hot mouth enveloped my cock. There was much about being a vampire that was less than ideal, but tonight, right here and right now, was a bright spot.

"Fuck. Your mouth is amazing. If you keep going, I'm going to come."

"That is the point." I swirled my tongue around his head and held his heavy balls in my hand.

"I want us to do..god, you're too formal for me. I want you fuck me until I explode. Wait, do vampires come?"

"Yes."

"Can it like get other vampires pregnant?"

"Seeing as we're dead, we're unable to create new life."

"Sweet. Not like either of us could get pregnant doing it, but just curious."

For a man swept up in sex, he was quite inquisitive.

I returned to my upside down position. This time, I turned Kilroy around. It was just like in the coffin, I didn't have to hide my erection.

"Yes. Give it to me."

I spat on my cock and smacked it against his hole.

"Wait. Do we need condoms?"

"Since we're dead, we're unable to carry or transfer diseases."

"Score!" He pumped a victorious fist, twisting his neck to look at me. "I always hated condoms. I mean, I totally got why they were necessary, and I'm pro safe-sex, but they were a bitch and a half to put on."

"And to answer your next question, vampires are naturally lubricated." His face lit up as if I told him he never had to wait in line again. "Some believe it's the blood diet."

"Sweet."

"Speaking of sweet." I entered his tight, pink opening. He clenched his whole body and let out a gasp as I filled him up with my thickness. I buried my face in his wild blond hair.

"Fuck. I was missing out as a human." He jutted his ass out so he could take more of me. I slid in and out of him slowly, taking my time, savoring every second and praying that I never forgot how this felt no matter how long I lived.

I wrapped an arm across his sweaty chest and pumped into his opening.

"Shit. You are hitting...everything." He flung his head back. "Holy shit, you are a sex god."

"I've had *centuries* of practice." There was a period in the late 1800s when to numb the boredom of eternity, I fucked my way across Europe. I was no sex god but a mere immortal.

Kilroy bent forward and grabbed onto the metal rods in front of him. His flexibility was impressive. And I had a delicious view of his ass. The angle allowed me to go deeper, fucking him with ferocious passion.

"Feels so good. Don't stop," Kilroy said between thrusts. "I'm so close."

I didn't want us to finish this way. I wanted to look into his eyes, watch his face go hazy with orgasm.

I brought us down and moved us against the wall. He wrapped his legs around me and let out a pleasurable moan as I re-entered him.

"Hey," he said softly.

"How do you do?" I tucked a lock of wayward blond hair behind his ear.

"Magnus?"

"Yes?"

"Is it corny to say I'm having a really good time?"

The laughter and smiles that I watched others experience, snapshots of joy that were as foreign a feeling as taking one's pulse, were now washing over me. My chest was full of light as if a cluster of fireflies took hold, and in that moment, I realized that this was what being happy felt like.

22

KILROY

Whatever hesitations I might've had about same-sex sex vanished when I kissed Magnus. I used to be nervous while waiting in line to ride a roller coaster. Every single time, the same nerves. But once the ride started, my fear was replaced with excitement. *Oh, yeah, this was going to be awesome*, I'd think.

Sex with Magnus was the most epic roller coaster ride.

"Are you alright?" he asked, his voice tender. "You seem deep in thought."

"Sorry. I was thinking about roller coasters."

He cocked his head, not sure if that was a good thing or a bad thing.

I sunk down, letting his thick cock breach my hole again and again. It was strange, new. There were physical feelings that I'd never felt; my body was being used in a different and creative way.

Magnus went deeper, and my body went from Strange-huh? to Strange-YES.

"Whoa." A moan of lust escaped me. I loved the feeling

of Magnus taking over my body, steadying me with his strong arms. His eyes turned red, lust lashing through him.

"Are you–"

"I am so alright it's not even funny." I threw my head back and let out a guttural groan from deep inside. I pulled my legs tighter around him. "This feels so good."

Magnus went a little faster. I could tell that he wanted to push it to the max, but he was taking it slow for me. He filled me up and stretched me, hitting every pleasure center I had.

"Shit." I threw my head back. "Need it."

That gave Magnus the green light. He picked up the pace, full-on fucking me. His thighs slapped against my ass. We were freaking levitating.

Literally.

I looked down, and our feet weren't touching the ground. Magnus had one hand balanced on the desk chair, holding us up. Superstrength FTW.

He unleashed a grunt that shook the furniture. He pulled my hair hard and licked my neck as he pounded into my tight opening.

Heat rose between us. His eyes got redder. Ravenous.

I gave him a nod. *Give me everything you got.*

Magnus flung us against the door, staying inside me, my legs around him as tight as they could get. He turned us upside down, and the new position managed to find another pleasure center. Holy shit, did it ever. I was a huffing, puffing, moaning mess of a vampire.

Our room turned into a pinball course, and we were the ball. He stayed inside me as we flung each other from one wall to the other, from floor to ceiling. I shoved us against the coffin; he slammed us into the bathroom sink. Red and lust and heat burned every inch of the room. Every picture on the wall hung on for dear life.

Through all of our extreme fucking, we never took our eyes off each other. We were locked in, the intensity sizzling on every sliver of my skin.

"Fill me the fuck up," I said as I shoved us to the floor and sat on his dick.

Who knew I had this kind of longing for some D? My fingers thread in his chest hair; his manliness made my toes curl.

"Magnus, I'm gonna come."

My hole clenched around his cock as I panted wildly. My load shot out, hitting his stomach, chest, and most impressively, his face.

"Come inside me," I ordered. Was that okay for vampires? I really didn't care at this point. We were already dead. What was the worst that could happen?

A few more thrusts and Magnus did as asked, draining his cock in my ass.

I sunk down the side of the coffin like the spent corpse I was, my body gelatinous. Magnus's cheeks were flush with afterglow.

He cleaned us off with his discarded shirt.

"Wow. If I'd known sex could be that mind-blowing, I would've become a vampire years ago."

"You're welcome." Magnus's lips curled up in a pleased smile.

"One more question," I said while catching my breath.

"Yes?"

"When you become a vampire, do you become a virgin all over again?"

"I do not know of a formal ruling on the matter, so I believe it comes down to personal choice."

"Then Magnus." I patted his thick thigh, skimming my

palm over the dusting of hair. "Congratulations are in order. You just popped my vampire cherry."

23

MAGNUS

We might've fucked like demons, but we slept like angels. When I woke the next evening, Kilroy was still nestled in my arms.

I had slept well the previous days, but this time, my slumber was so peaceful I was liable to slip into a coma.

I didn't know if he was up or not. But that didn't stop me from kissing along his neck, letting my fang graze the skin. I never wanted to get up. I could spend literal eternity in this coffin with this vampire.

Kilroy stirred under me. The first thing he did was wiggle his butt, sending a bolt of lust into my stomach. If he kept that up, we'd destroy the coffin.

"Morning," he said through his raspy, sleep-drenched voice.

"Technically afternoon." I kissed his shoulder. It was a little after four. The sun in Iceland had just gone down after five measly hours of daylight.

Kilroy turned to me, a dreamy gaze sparkling in his eye, and it was all for me.

He was perfect. This moment was perfect.

And just as quickly, doubt crept in like a slayer waiting for the ideal time to pounce.

What if he just took last night at face value? What if he merely saw it as a night of combustible, wall-shaking sex, a natural extension of the flirtation building between us?

Kilroy had his whole afterlife ahead of him. He probably wanted to explore and indulge. He was naturally curious. The man had traveled to the ends of the earth on a whim to surf. Why wouldn't he want to spend eternity playing the field?

I couldn't blame him. Several vampires had that mindset. I was one of the weird ones who was constantly searching for his person.

Kilroy could easily sit up, declare that he adored vampire sex, and planned to fuck his way through the hotel. How could I counter that?

"What are you thinking?" he asked. "You're staring very intently at the coffin lid."

"I thought someone had rudely carved their initials into the wood. This is a custom piece of furniture, not a tree in the woods at summer camp."

"I don't see anything." He leaned his head against mine. Oh how I wanted to stare into the stars with him night after night, feeling the rhythmic breathing lift and lower his chest.

"I assume you have plans for tonight," I said, willing myself not to get more attached to this cute vampire. "You probably have an itinerary, things you want to explore." I scrambled for an example, and I remembered the photograph. "You wanted to see the Black Fortress."

"What?" Surprise lit up his face.

"I accidentally saw it written down on a photograph..."

"Right. Yeah. I was going to check it out sometime."

"I wasn't trying to snoop. The picture fell on the floor and..."

"No, I get it."

"Make sure to go late at night lest you run into any guests. And don't stay for long and make yourself vulnerable."

"Copy that."

"Splendid. Well, I don't want to take up your entire vacation. That would be unfair of me." I sat up, pushed open the coffin cover. The glow of the chandelier above, which fortunately remained intact, cast a harsh light.

I stood up and climbed out. This was for the best. We consummated the tension between us. It was best to leave things before my feelings for Kilroy developed any further. Let him enjoy his plans.

I put on fresh underwear and pants, pulled a crisp fresh shirt from the dresser drawer. I turned around to find Kilroy watching me with a curious expression.

"What?" I asked.

"Nothing. It's just that I didn't take you for a hit-it-and-quit-it kinda guy."

"I—what? I am unaware of that expression."

"Well, you hit it." Kilroy gestured to himself. "And now you're quitting it."

I didn't appreciate being called a quitter, even if Kilroy's description had kernels of truth. And I'd hoped that what we shared last night was more than hitting it to him.

"It's usually customary that when you rail someone, you take him out to brunch the next morning." Kilroy quirked a playful eyebrow. My insides were quickly spiraling into a mess, yet he seemed to be having a ball.

"Forgive me. I'm not one of those vampires who engages in casual sex. Or at least, it's been a few decades. I don't want you to feel uncomfortable and think that you have to placate me with a post-coital meal. I'm fine. Chill, as one might say." I shoved my feet into my boots.

To my surprise, Kilroy had a look of dejection flash across his luminous face.

"Magnus, can I ask you a question?"

"Yes."

"Do you feel uncomfortable?"

"No. Absolutely not." I looked down and realized my shirt's buttons were off and my boots were on the wrong feet.

"Can I ask you another question?"

"Certainly."

"What would you say if I told you that I don't feel uncomfortable and this wasn't casual sex for me?"

My heart clenched in my chest. His statement was a sliver of light shining under a doorway. "Is that how you feel?"

He nodded yes. "I played this game so many times when I was a human. I was the master of hitting it and quitting it. I could duck out like a champ. And I ended my human life alone."

That was a benefit to eventually forgetting your human life; you didn't have to live with those regrets. Kilroy's lips pouted with deep thought and rough reflection. The only thing worse than living your human life alone was living in eternity by oneself.

"Kilroy, if I may be honest, I would like us to go to breakfast." My throat wobbled as I uttered this final word: "Together."

Light returned to the surfer's expression.

"I'd like that, too."

"Good." I nodded as if this were normal business, but inside me, fireworks were going off.

"You know what I'd also like?" A mischievous smile curled on Kilroy's lips. "Some batshit crazy vampire morning sex."

"Technically afternoon sex."

"Just go with it, dude." He pulled me by the shirt back into the coffin.

24

KILROY

After another whirlwind fornication which left the coffin a little worse for wear, we enjoyed breakfast in the hotel restaurant. We split French toast drizzled with a strawberry and blood infused syrup. I never thought I could enjoy fruit on my French toast. I was always a chocolate-chip pancakes kinda guy. It looked like Magnus was changing me for good.

While eating, Alvin and Simon stopped by our table. Alvin's plate had French toast covered in a mountain of whipped cream. It reminded me of sledding yesterday.

"Did you guys hear about the slayers that were found frozen to death?" Simon asked. His tie dye shirt popped against the dreary decor.

Magnus and I shared a pretend look of surprise.

"Is that so?" Magnus asked, playing it super cool.

"Einar said they got closer to the hotel than any other human before them." Concern flashed on Simon's usually even-keeled face. Even I got spooked.

"They weren't that close," Magnus said.

A knowing smile took over Alvin and Simon's lips.

"We heard that a vampire had already gotten to them and enjoyed a snack," Alvin said. "Thanks for sharing."

"You weren't around. It would've gone to waste." Magnus shrugged.

"Finders keepers?" I laughed.

"Well, the next time idiot stakers try and make their way up here, we call dibs." Alvin nodded to emphasize his point.

"Fair is fair," I said.

"Since there are slayers around, we may lay low and hang out around the hotel," Simon said.

"That's not a bad idea." Magnus wiped the corners of his mouth with his napkin.

"But why do we have to lock ourselves away? Maybe we can broker a peace between humans and vampires."

Magnus, Alvin, and Simon traded looks that told me where they stood on that idea. A big, fat nope. They studied me as if I was legit crazy.

"Did you break into my weed stash?" Simon cocked an eyebrow at me.

"What? Why is that so hard to imagine?"

"Oh, I don't know. Maybe ask Native Americans how it went for them," Alvin said.

I turned to Magnus, hoping to have one person in my corner.

"I'm with them," he said.

"We admire your youthful spirit, but that's never going to happen." Alvin gave my hand a condescending pat. "It's not worth getting upset over. Life is too long to get caught up on things outside your control. I went to this vampire zen retreat last year that I highly recommend."

"And I can get my bong from my room. Unless you already broke into my stash." Simon continued to cock a suspicious eyebrow my way.

"We're fine." Magnus gave my leg a supportive squeeze under the table.

Maybe if vampires and humans were around each other more, we could learn to coexist. People evolved. This wasn't the 1960s or 1800s. Something told me to keep this thought to myself as the others wouldn't understand.

"Have a good breakfast!" Magnus waved goodbye.

"Sorry about that," I said once they were gone.

"I understand the frustration. It's all still new for you."

"So what did you want to do tonight?" I asked, ready to change the subject.

"I haven't given it much thought."

"As much as I'd love to have sex all night long, we should probably do something outside the hotel room."

"Probably," he said, a flicker of red in his eyes. "We can go sledding again. There's a treacherous mountain with more zigs and zags."

"I'm game."

"Did you have anything planned when you came here?" he asked.

My eyes shifted to our French toast for an uncomfortable beat. I was providing the awkward vibes. Magnus deserved the truth, but I wasn't ready for that.

"Nope. I'm not really into planning. When I used to surf, I'd find a beach and book a plane ticket that day."

"That must've been expensive."

I shrugged and shoved a piece of French toast in my mouth. "Not like I needed to save for retirement. What about you? What were you supposed to be doing before I crashed your vacay?"

"It's customary to talk, then eat."

"Noted," I said mid-chew.

"I came to enjoy the peace and quiet of the mountains, eat some delicious food, and have some reflection."

"Doing the whole *Eat Pray Love* thing?"

"In a manner of speaking, I suppose so."

"Well, the way you were calling out God's name last night, I'd say you got the pray part down." I lifted my eyebrows in a cocky smirk. "So what should we do around the hotel that isn't sex?"

Magnus tapped his fork and knife. "Actually, there was something I was meaning to do."

"Where are you taking me?"

Magnus led us down a narrow hallway on the top floor that started off nice but soon turned creepy once we went through a door marked DO NOT ENTER. Cobwebs stretched from wall to wall. Weathered paint chipped on the ceiling. It seemed like a maze that would lead to a dead-end.

"If this is part of a plan to have me killed, could you do this in a nicer part of the hotel. Perhaps a corner of the lobby?"

Magnus said nothing.

We reached a thick, metal door, also marked DO NOT ENTER. Magnus didn't strike me as a guy who ignored DO NOT ENTER signs.

He pushed open the door, which creaked with a dire need for WD-40. We stepped onto a small balcony that overlooked…

"Holy shit. Is that a frozen waterfall?" My mouth gaped open. The waterfall defied the laws of nature. It was frozen in time. The icy gush of water fell off a cliff and stopped in midair. "That is so freaking cool."

"I agree." Magnus marveled with equal astonishment as me.

"How have I never heard about a frozen waterfall?"

"The elevation is too high for humans. And because it's tucked behind the larger mountains, nobody's found out. It's our secret."

"How did a large body of water survive up here and then freeze mid-waterfall?" I really wish I hadn't slacked off in my high school earth science class.

"My best guess is that it's millions of years old, and as the continents shifted, it slowly got colder until it froze."

"What if it started as a waterfall in the rainforest?"

"That's possible. After all this time, there were still things out there that were unknowable to me." He wrapped his arm around my shoulders.

"Do other vampires know about this?" I tilted my head back slightly to look at him.

"I don't believe so. As you could probably tell, the door to this balcony rarely gets opened."

"Yeah, at first I thought you were taking me into a dungeon."

"Dungeons are by design located underground or beneath things, not on the top floor."

"Maybe it was a special dungeon? This is way better." I played with the puka shells on my necklace, stringing my finger back and forth as I gazed into the frozen unknown. Nature really was 100% that bitch.

"Someone had known about it, hence the balcony, but I take it they're long gone," he said.

"I can see why you like to come here to think."

I interlocked his fingers with mine, but I got a sense he wasn't feeling it.

He cleared his throat. "We discovered it by accident. Years ago."

We.

Magnus's face went solemn. I kept having to remember that he'd lived several lifetimes already.

"Gunnar was looking for an ice machine because the one on our floor was broken. 'Gunnar, if you want ice, we can just go outside.' He could be stubborn like that. Once an idea came into his head, he couldn't be swayed."

I smiled. Gunnar and I were plucked from the same tree.

"I don't remember how we wound up in this hallway. We were on what one might call a wild goose chase. But I'll never forget, or I hope I'll never forget, the first time we opened this door. It took us a few seconds to see the waterfall at first through the snow. The glint of moonlight hit the ice sheen and made it glitter in some otherworldly fashion.

"We were shocked that nobody knew about this. When we mentioned it to Einar, he called us crazy for thinking there was a frozen waterfall. He said we had to be seeing things. So Gunnar and I didn't tell anyone else. It was our secret."

He stared out at the ice, so obviously lost in his memories. I hoped he didn't forget them. Magnus had been in love, and I liked to believe the heart was better than the mind about remembering things. Love made life worth living. Love for others, love for our work, love of nature.

I brought his hand to my mouth for a soft kiss. "You miss him."

He nodded. "I lost him about three years ago. But the wound hasn't completely healed."

I saw that every time he tensed up talking about humans. I understood why he had no interest in coexisting with them.

"Gunnar always wanted me to be happy whether that was with him or someone else. He'd want me to move on, not because life was short but because it was long. Forever. Too long to spend it in mourning."

Gunnar was wise beyond his years. He got it.

I gazed deep into Magnus's eyes, communicating how I felt about him where words would fail. We'd only known each other a few days, but I'd never felt this kind of connection with anyone. Maybe being undead unlocked things within me, fears that kept me from truly loving others.

I turned to the waterfall.

"Hello, Gunnar!" I waved at the ice. "How's the after-afterlife?"

"Vampires don't believe in reincarnation."

"Excuse me, I'm in the middle of a conversation." I rolled my eyes at the waterfall. "Gunnar, it's great to meet you. My name's Kilroy. You can call me K or K-Dog. But not Roy. I'm not really a Roy kinda guy. You get it, right?"

The waterfall continued to stay frozen.

"Gunnar, you seem like a cool guy. Thank you for finding this place and for taking care of Magnus all those years." I put up my hand to do an aside to the waterfall. "The guy can be a little uptight."

"I'm not uptight. I'm fastidious and particular."

I returned to his conversation. "See what I'm talking about."

"I could be fun. Gunnar, back me up. Wait, why on earth am I conversing with a waterfall?"

I shook my head and smiled at the waterfall, as if Gunnar and I were both thinking "Classic Magnus."

"Gunnar, I want you to know that I'm going to take good care of Magnus." I dipped my hands into my pockets. Magnus might've been technically right about no after-

afterlife, but I felt Gunnar's spirit around us. "I wanted to introduce myself, and I'm here if you ever wanted to chat. But you don't have to worry about Magnus. He's in good hands."

I gave the waterfall, and the spirit of Gunnar, one more nod.

I knew that Magnus's heart would always hold Gunnar, which it should. But I hoped that it was big enough for me, too.

"You didn't need to get permission to date me," Magnus said.

"Well, your dad's not around."

"I just want you to know that I'm not trying to replace anyone." I looked down at my sneakers. "I wish my stepdad had said something like this when he married my mom. It might've stopped me and him from butting heads."

"Oh. I didn't know."

"I don't talk about my real family for a reason. That's why I decided to travel around the world looking for the perfect surf. Any place was better than home."

"At least you found your ChoBros."

I could tell he hated saying that word because it wasn't standard English, but I appreciated that he did. "Thank you for bringing me here."

We kissed softly, lust replaced with something deeper and more intimate. We took time to admire the waterfall, leaning our heads on each other and savoring the peace of watching nature at work.

"Let's get on with it." I nodded to the door. "The night is young."

25

MAGNUS

"Happy New Year's Eve!" Kilroy whispered in my ear when we awoke the next evening. He pulled me close to him in his big spoon. Sleeping in a too-small coffin had its perks.

I wiped sleep from my eyes. After visiting the waterfall last night, we laid low and relaxed. We cuddled by the fireplace and drank hot cocoa. We helped put together a giant puzzle that took up two giant tables in the lobby. Later, we enjoyed a piano concert by a vampire who used to run in the same circles as Beethoven and would've been a famous composer too, had he not been bitten.

Throughout the night, Kilroy had a notepad with him, and he seemed to be taking notes. About what, I was clueless. Whenever I asked, he said he was doing research but refused to divulge about what he was researching. The times I tried to peek over his shoulder, he used his enhanced speed to slam his notebook shut. Currently, said notebook sat at the bottom of his suitcase. Even if I could reach it, he'd be too fast and would slap it shut again. He told me he'd show it to me in time.

I had all the time in the world. If only he could be more specific.

I let the thought go when he pulled me closer and kissed up my neck. We snuggled and cuddled in our coffin. I didn't take myself for the kind of person who used words like snuggle and cuddle, but there was a first for everything.

We lay like that for a while before I insisted we get up.

"I know it's technically New Year's Eve, but there are no planned festivities for tonight." I drifted my finger down the curves of his chest.

He shrugged in that carefree way of his that said everything would be alright. "I don't know. I still think that making it to a new year is worth celebrating. Another year older."

"Celebrating another year older when you are incapable of aging seems rather pointless, don't you think?"

"You get to kiss someone at midnight."

"Midnight is the middle of the day for us."

"That means you get to kiss them more." Kilroy kissed along my arm, but despite how scintillating his lips felt, it still did not muster any further New Year's Eve enthusiasm in me.

"New Year's Eve is a human holiday."

"Why can't it be both?"

I smiled at him and enveloped him in a sweeping kiss, mostly to end this conversation.

"What should we do tonight?" I asked. "We can go sledding again."

Kilroy smiled back, but there was something different, something not quite there. "Is it cool if we do our own thing tonight? I was thinking about how you like your alone time for reflection, and that might be good for me, if that's cool."

I stammered for an answer. I didn't expect Kilroy to want

alone time for reflection. Being with him made me want to spend more time with him, especially since our vacation was coming to an end.

"Of course that's cool. This is your vacation. You should get to spend it as you want."

"I don't want to spend my eternity alone. Just one night. Not even. Only a few hours." He tipped my chin to give me a kiss. "I want to send off New Year's Eve in my own way."

I breathed a sigh of relief. I had to get out of my head sometimes, which was difficult since as an immortal being, I had a lot of time to think.

"I'm going to grab us some breakfast and bring it back to the room." I hopped out of the coffin and got dressed, which was very difficult to do since a naked Kilroy was right there.

I whistled as I practically tap danced downstairs to the lobby. Einar was going through files at the front desk.

I tapped his bell a few times in beat to the song playing in my head.

"Good afternoon, Einar."

"Magnus. You seem to be in a good mood."

"Of course I'm in a good mood. I'm on vacation." I gave the bell one more joyful ring before Einar smartly removed it from the counter. "I wanted to thank you and Reynar for your help the other night with the theater."

"My pleasure. How did the evening go?"

"Very well."

"And still not a date, yes?" His bushy eyebrows shot up. Ninety-year-olds could still be sarcastic bastards.

"It might've veered into date territory."

"The guest in the room next to yours asked me if there was an avalanche the other night because the wall was shaking so much. You wouldn't happen to know about that, would you?" Einar kept a straight face and waited for my response.

I brushed a molecule of dust off the counter. "I would not. I've slept like a baby."

"Well, I'm glad the roommate arrangement has worked out and that you and Mr. Kilroy have managed to get along."

This was a game of chicken. Einar was waiting for me to break.

"We have been getting along." Dare I let Einar into my friend circle? "In fact, to be perfectly honest, we might be ending this vacation as more than roommates."

His baggy eyes blew open. His spunky younger self was still in there under the wrinkles.

"Magnus, that's wonderful! I always hoped you'd find someone else after Gunnar. I think he'd like Mr. Kilroy."

"Me, too. Can I ask you a question?"

"Of course." He moved his files to the side.

"Kilroy said he wanted to spend some time alone tonight. Does that sound…"

"Like something you need to worry about?" He proudly shook his head no. "Not at all. From vampires I've spoken with in my career, the first year is almost the hardest. It's a long time ago for you, so you probably don't remember, but it can be a hard transition. There's a lot to process."

Kilroy had only been a vampire for a few months. I had to keep reminding myself of that.

"He cares for you. I see the way you two are. You both care very much about each other. And it's still new, but I see something there."

Einar always knew how to take care of guests, no matter our issue. Leaky sinks, post-coital anxiety. It was all the same to him.

"Evening!" Reynar stopped by. He held a large sign in his hands. "How did the movie work out?"

I gave him two big thumbs up, Kilroy style.

"You have the sign?" Einar asked him.

"Yep." Reynar plunked it on the counter.

A sinking feeling hit me as I read the sign.

ATTENTION: STAY AWAY FROM THE BLACK FORTRESS. HIGH PRESENCE OF HUMANS TONIGHT.

"What's going on?" I asked Reynar. "Humans never go to the Black Fortress at night."

"I just got word that a massive outdoor New Year's Eve party is being held there. They're going to have music, heat lamps, and dancing. And I'm guessing lots of liquor and marijuana. They're expecting hundreds of humans."

"A New Year's Eve party?" I asked, dread filling my bones.

Reynar nodded yes. He pulled up the information on his mobile and handed it over.

"People from all over the world are coming in for it. It's being thrown by this international surfing group. They thought it'd be fun for the surfing community to meet up at the coldest place on earth." He turned to Einar and laughed. "Me, I'd rather be on the beach."

26

KILROY

I didn't have a mirror, so I had to go by instinct. And my instincts said I was having a good hair day. I wore my best Hawaiian shirt and board shorts, ones they'd recognize instantly.

When I stepped out of the bathroom, Magnus was standing in the middle of the room stone-faced.

"Hey. Are they no longer serving breakfast?"

"Don't go."

He was ultra serious. A weird feeling brewed in my stomach.

"To breakfast? Uh oh, did Reynar undercook the eggs?"

"Don't go to the ice castle. Don't go to the party."

I looked down at my photograph hanging between his fingers. I opened my mouth, but I was out of lies.

"I can explain, Magnus."

"That's why you came to Iceland. Your ChoBros are going to this party, and you wanted to see them."

"That wasn't the entire reason. I knew it was happening, and then I was looking at Iceland and found this hotel and thought it was fate. I've been deciding whether or not to go this whole week."

"You never said anything. You've been lying to me."

"I'm sorry. I hate lying, and I hate lying to you."

"Yet you still did it."

"Because I knew you'd freak out."

"You're not going," he said with absolute firmness, his voice deep and grave. Usually, I'd be turned on having him speak to me like that, but not in this context.

"It's going to be sick."

"I take it that's a good thing, but you're still not going." He walked in front of the door as if he were preparing to block it. Was he my stepfather telling me what to do? Frustration rose in my throat.

"I'm going," I said defiantly.

"Kilroy."

"Why don't you come with me? It'll be fun! There's going to be ice luges and a DJ. You can meet my old surfer buddies."

"Will we take a selfie before or after they drive a stake through our hearts?"

"C'mon. They're not like that. They're good guys. They're a big part of my life."

"They *were* a part of your life, but not anymore."

"You'd like them," I said, ignoring his dig.

"Kilroy, you can't go to that party." He didn't let up. He was like a machine.

"Why not?"

"Because you're a vampire!"

"I know your rules about not hanging with humans, but these are my peeps. They're not going to freak out. Most of them will probably be too high to notice anything off."

"Yes, they will. When humans see a vampire, they panic. Their instinct is to slay us."

Was he right? I was starting to question whether I could trust my ChoBros. They were my family. They were all about peace. They weren't killers.

"Hashtag not all humans."

"Yes all humans!" He pushed himself against the door, keeping it shut. "Kilroy, I know you want to see your friends, but you have to understand that you are no longer Kilroy the human to them. You are a vampire. They won't recognize you; they will only see a vampire that they want to kill."

"There's going to be dark lighting. They won't notice that I'm pale and have fangs." I could tell my attitude was only angering Magnus. I had a bad tendency to lean on humor during tense times.

"And what about you? You're going to surround yourself with humans pumping fresh, tasty blood? What happens if you get ravenous?"

"I won't eat my friends. Gross."

"Kilroy, listen to me!" His eyes were wild with terror. I lurched back scared.

"Magnus, I think you're overreacting. It's been how long since you were around humans? They've evolved. They don't carry pitchforks anymore, just iPhones. And maybe you had bad encounters, but that doesn't mean all humans are like that."

"Bad encounters? Getting chased by vicious slayers and listening to them slaughter my lover is not what I'd call a bad encounter."

"I'm sorry. I didn't mean that." I hung my head, feeling like an asshole. I wanted to be sensitive to Magnus, but I also wanted to give my ChoBros a chance. "I believe that there are good humans out there."

"Humans show kindness and grace to fellow humans, but not to vampires. We are a curse upon the earth according to them, a malignant tumor in the universe's grand plan that must be extracted at once."

"What about Einar and Reynar? They're humans. They're cool with us."

"They come from a special lineage of people who were bred to coexist with vampires."

"Well, maybe my friends have some of their DNA. I can have them do a 23andMe test."

"Not before they hold you down and plunge a sharp, wooden object through your heart! We survive by keeping our distance."

I shuffled to the coffin and sat on the lid. "I traveled the world with these guys. We shared our deepest secrets and greatest fears. Our bonds were forged on the open seas. They saved my life over and over after every wipeout. They're my family. Are you telling me that my own family will want to kill me the second they see me?"

He nodded yes without a second of hesitation. Maybe it wasn't the best idea for me to spend time with a vampire who had such a negative view of the world.

"These men, these ChoBros...they loved the human Kilroy. Their brotherly love for you is buried in a cemetery." He heaved out a sigh, dreading what he was about to say. "They're not your family anymore."

"So what are you saying? I just don't have family anymore? I have to walk the earth knowing that there are people who love me who I can never see again?" Frustration rose in my throat. I didn't choose to get bitten on the beach. I was only twenty-five. I had so much more life to live.

"I'm sorry," he said quietly.

"Just because you've been around for centuries, you

think you're some know-it-all. Well, I have a newsflash for you, Magnus. You're not as smart as you think you are. There's a lot about the world and people that you don't know. You don't know jack shit about my friends."

"I know humans."

"You think they're all the same. You think they're all out to kill us."

"They are!"

"How do you know? Outside of Einar and Reynar, I'm guessing you haven't spoken to a human in a long time. Hell, you barely talk to vampires. You look down on everyone from your lonely mountaintop and think you know better." The words spewed out of me.

"Kilroy, you're angry right now. I understand."

"Magnus. Please move."

Aside from his trembling lip, he didn't move. His hand gripped the doorknob tight.

"I miss them." My voice wobbled for a beat. I wanted to see their smiles in person, not on a flat photograph. I wanted to feel the warmth of their hugs and hear the hearty cackle of their laughter. We could be together one more time. "I just want five minutes with them. Five minutes to let them know I'm okay, then I'll go."

"I can't let you do that." He shook his head no, his face impenetrable.

"Then I'm sorry, Magnus." I leapt to the window, opened the hatch, and I was gone. Faster than a bat out of hell.

27

KILROY

The Black Fortress was on fire tonight. Metaphorical fire. Wait...could lava be set on fire?

Lights of all different colors illuminated the space and shined into the sky. Music pulsed from between the rocks. Lines of cars were parked at the entrance.

From my current distance, it resembled a medieval castle. People partied in the open space, and others had climbed the rocks to more private areas. One rock stretching up had a viewing ledge with a ladder attached. It reminded me of a medieval tower.

Tonight though, instead of Rapunzel letting down her hair, it was a guy letting down a shower of puke.

Now *this* was a party.

I hadn't been to a real rager since I was a human. Vampire fiestas were a more subdued joint. I experienced that familiar anticipation swirl inside me as I got closer to the doors. Anything and everything could happen at a party. I had so many sweet memories of ragers past, and this one promised to be just as bitchin'.

Even if I was a vampire.

I kept thinking of my argument with Magnus, which put a damper on my excitement. I considered myself an even-keeled guy. The waves mellowed me out. I'd never gotten angry like that with someone, especially someone I cared about. But I was scared that Magnus was right, that my ChoBros wanted nothing to do with me. Was I going to be alone in eternity?

The pulsing music got me back in the festive mood. Things were going to work out. Things tended to work out for me. Well, minus getting turned into a vampire. But even that wasn't a bust.

I got closer to the Black Fortress, approaching from the side. The sound of tons of people gave me slight pause. It also made me lightheaded in an unexpected way. My stomach rumbled—nay, earthquaked—under my shirt.

Shit.

When was the last time I had some blood? I stormed out of the room before Magnus and I could go to breakfast.

I could hear Magnus judging me from the hotel. *Vampires need blood, dude, or else they become crazy maniacs.* Magnus would say it in his sophisticated way that was totally adorable.

The guy in the rock tower threw up again. When I glanced up at the girl holding his hair back, I noticed it was Amelia, a core member of my surfing crew, the token female ChoBro.

Then I realized that the thrower upper was Biff, another ChoBro who surfed the most epic wave in Kuala Lumpur three years ago. It was so brutal that it ripped off his swimsuit.

Entering a party through the front was such a basic human move. I took it to the next level.

I leapt up the side of the rock. It would be a fun surprise

for them. Like how I surprised Magnus outside our hotel room window. I hung just beyond the ledge's visibility.

Biff was on his knees moaning in pain. Amelia rubbed his back like a good nurse.

"Dude, what did Kilroy always say?" she said.

My ears perked up at my name.

"Wine coolers are no joke," they said in unison. Biff talked into his hand, but I could still hear his monotone voice. It was odd seeing them in chunky sweaters and corduroys instead of T-shirts and shorts.

"That was a great night," she said, smiling up at the stars.

I remembered saying that. We were at a bonfire celebrating an epic ride in Guam of all places. It was an island in the middle of the Pacific Ocean that was US territory, so we could use dollars and there was McDonalds. I had too many wine coolers, thinking that they were like candy. Cut to me emptying my stomach into a bush later that night. One of our ChoBros Dirk used to be a paramedic and said he never heard vomiting that intense. I took it as a badge of honor.

"I miss Kilroy," Biff said.

"Me, too." She stroked her long nails over his back. Amelia gave the best massages.

"I'm right here," I said softly, stepping onto the ledge.

"Did someone say something?" Biff asked. He was too out of it to lift his head.

A mix of conflicting emotions flashed on Amelia's face when she turned around and saw me, as if she were deciding how to react. Her mouth made an O shape. Her eyes went super big. All I could see was shock crystallizing her features.

"Hey, Mel. It's me."

She was a deer in my headlights. She stood up and took a step closer.

"You know how much I love New Years." I managed a weak smile. Her silence and fixed stare were freaking me out. "I can explain."

I flashed her my most Kilroy smile, the smile that got me out of parking tickets and penalties for late bill payments.

Her face shifted and the tiniest glimmer of recognition snuck up in her eyes, the whisper of a hairline smile began to curl on her lips.

And then Biff screamed.

He screamed so loud and at such a high-pitch it was as if someone squeezed all the testosterone out of his nuts. It was blood-curdling.

Mmmm blood.

Whatever drunk pre-hangover he was suffering through vanished. He stumbled in front of Amelia and continued screaming bloody murder.

Mmmm blood.

Stop that!

"Biff it's me!" I yelled back, but my voice was no match for his wail.

He flung his cell phone at me. Then his plastic bottle of water.

"HELP!" he yelled down the ladder at the loud mass of partygoers.

My instincts kicked in and in a flash, I was across the ledge pushing him away from the ladder.

"Biff! It's me!"

"Vampire! Vampire! Monster! Somebody help us!"

I smelled a stench and looked down at the trail of urine soaking his shorts. Biff and I had surfed for years. He had to give me mouth-to-mouth once and had no problem putting his lips on me. Now I made him piss his pants.

We were ChoBros. Didn't he recognize me? What did I look like to him? Was I a vision from his worst dreams?

The sound of footsteps charging up the ladder broke me from my thoughts.

"Biff, what the hell is going on?" Damian said. "I could hear you above the…"

Biff pointed a shaky hand at me.

Damian and I had grown up together. He'd been there for me when I left home. He'd gotten me into surfing. There was nothing I couldn't come to him with. We were brothers in every way except blood, he used to say. He was the ChoBro that had lived up to the "Bro" part the most.

And now he glared at me, shooting me the ugliest, most disgusted look I could imagine someone giving another person.

"What the fuck are you?"

"It's me. Kilroy."

Damian screamed, the same wail as Biff. Had he not heard me say my name? What did I sound like to humans? He ripped off his cross necklace and waved it in my face.

"Get out of here!"

I smacked his cross to the floor. Damian used to say that organized religion was bullshit.

"I'm not the devil. I'm your friend!" I yelled, my voice hoarse with desperation.

He and Biff screamed again. Biff found an object to throw that could actually cause damage. He hurled a piece of black rock at my head, making me stumble back.

"Shit! What do we do?" Biff asked, hands shaking.

"I was reading up on this. I'd heard that vampires were in Iceland. We need to get a sharp piece of wood and jam it through his heart." Damian made the stabbing motion in my direction. "Kill this fucker dead."

I held back tears. Nobody wanted to see a monster cry.

"Guys!" Amelia jumped between them. She made eye contact with me and for a second, I saw my old friend.

Our moment was cut short by three buff Nordic guys charging into the room. They wore all black, which made their bright blond hair look almost white. Biff pulled Amelia back, away from the monster.

The Nordic guys snarled at me in perverse joy like dobermans guarding an evil lair finally about to have some fun.

"One of these were stupid enough to come here? Get them out of here," the tallest Nordic man said of my friends. His flowing blond hair, accent, and scowl reminded me of a *Die Hard* henchman. The other two behind him, one with a face full of acne and the other with a bulldog-looking grimace, moved like trained agents, shuffling my friends down the ladder. It would probably be the last time I ever saw them.

And my final memory would be of their screaming.

Mr. *Die Hard* pulled a stake from his back pocket. Did they all carry those around with them? Wasn't that a hazard? What if he accidentally fell?

"I'm going to enjoy this." His smile made whatever blood was left in me go cold. "Staking a vampire is one of my favorite things to do."

I was a nice guy. I went through life never making enemies. It was truly surreal to now have multiple people angling to murder me, staring at me with nothing but hate in their eyes.

"Fellas, c-can't we come to an understanding here?" I asked. "Please?"

But my words only seemed to fan the flames of their bloodlust. Fiery hate burned in their eyes. They stomped toward me, and my vampire instincts kicked in. I jumped off the ledge. I didn't see where I was going and landed on another piece of rock, scraping up my hand. I jumped to the next rock, then the other. It was a lot more fun doing this with Magnus and trees when I wasn't running for my life.

I slipped on an icy patch and tumbled to the ground. My shoulder and leg throbbed in unholy pain, and I couldn't shake it off. I did a quick check. My arms were gashed from the fall, but no blood in the wounds.

Blood.

I craved it.

Was that why my body felt weak and sluggish? I had to keep going. I ran through the field of rocks until the music was barely a gentle hum in the distance. Fear and bloodlust clouded my head, my brain caught in the middle of a battle. The hotel was a ways away, but maybe I'd run into another frozen body and get a needed infusion.

If only dead bodies grew on trees.

Wait. Why wasn't I turning myself into a bat? Vampire advantage numero uno.

I shut my eyes and prepared to transform when I felt a rope loop around my ankles and get so tight it broke the skin. I tumbled forward, unable to fight through the gravity pulling me down. I smacked my head on a rock and everything went black.

28

KILROY

When I came to, I was on the ground, my arms and legs tied to stakes. Panic climbed in my throat.

I tried to focus on getting home. I wanted to apologize to Magnus for not listening to him. I thought back on good times with my old friends.

The three Nordic guys dressed as cat burglars stood over me. Seeing them up close, I noticed a pin clipped to their jackets; the same logo was on the jacket of the frozen slayers I'd eaten.

Mr. *Die Hard* let out a venomous chuckle for his two backups. "Vampires are an interesting contradiction. They have enhanced strength and can turn into bats, but if you tie their ankles together, they become completely useless."

They brandished their freshly carved wooden stakes in their bare hands. My teeth chattered, not from the cold but from abject fear. I suddenly realized that I wasn't as immortal as I thought.

"Hey, dudes. Look, it's New Year's Eve. Why don't we do some shots and talk this over?" I tried to keep a jocular tone in the hopes of disarming them. I searched for the humanity in their eyes, but all I saw was black.

"A vampire who cracks jokes? That's a new one," said Mr. Acne. He couldn't have been older than eighteen. "We're here to send you back to hell where you belong."

I'd never had someone look at me with such pure hatred. Like I was evil. It made me wonder if they were right.

Did vampires go to hell after they'd been staked? Magnus would know. He knew everything. Fuck, I wished he were here.

Mr. *Die Hard* pulled out a pocket bible. "We are here in the name of God."

"Does God really want you killing on his behalf? Doesn't he tell you to love everyone?"

Mr. *Die Hard* ignored me and flipped through the pages to a dogeared passage. They dog-eared books? These people were truly sociopathic.

"Shit." He sliced his finger open with a nasty paper cut.

Blood oozed from the opening. My eyes lit up with overpowering hunger. I no longer cared that they wanted to kill me.

"Jacob, he's attacking!" Mr. Bulldog screamed and everything went into a blur. My muscles went full blast, and my arms began to lift from the ground. Blinded by my lust for blood, I didn't see Mr. Acne pick up a rock and smash it into my face.

I collapsed back down, the world spinning around me.

"I'm sorry," I uttered out, pain and dizziness gripping me. "Force...of habit."

"Hold him down," Mr. *Die Hard* said.

I thrashed wildly as the other two slayers sat on my arms. My injuries had inhibited my superstrength and I couldn't break free. I was getting close, kicking up my legs.

"Ancient demon, we have come here tonight to cleanse the earth of your kind."

"Have you already gotten through all the human criminals and abusers first?" I snapped.

Mr. *Die Hard* flashed an ugly smile of crooked teeth at the other two, almost impressed. "This one has a sense of humor."

"Silence, demon!" Mr. Acne said.

"I'm not a demon!"

They ground into my arm, pushing me further into the snow. I let out a howl of pain.

The point of the stake glimmered in the moonlight. This was it. Death.

Again.

Permanent, actual death.

I didn't remember how I felt when I got bitten on the beach. My mind went blank and the next thing I knew, I was lying on the sand rubbing my neck. Would it be the same here? The place where I was going, would I even remember how I got there? Would I remember being a vampire?

Would I remember Magnus and the frozen waterfall and surfing on volcanoes?

"Please," I whimpered out, my last shot. They ignored me. I wasn't a person. I was a thing to be killed, a bug to be stepped on.

Mr. *Die Hard* raised his stake. I shut my eyes and braced for impact.

Yet it never came.

Or maybe it did and this was some twisted version of hell?

Mr. Bulldog unleashed a terrified scream that reminded me of Biff. The weight on my body seemed to lift.

I opened one eye. No stake to be seen. Yet I watched Mr.

Bulldog and Mr. Acne fly across the night sky like darts, landing against a boulder. It took me a moment to realize they were thrown.

I followed their screams to the spot in the snow where Mr. *Die Hard* was on his knees, head tilted so his neck was exposed, Magnus standing over him.

29

MAGNUS

"What are you doing here?" I asked him, my voice coming out in a feral growl.

The human quivered in my grip.

"W-we came here t-to cleanse the earth."

"Then buy a broom." I bared my fangs. Anger lashed through me. All I saw was white.

The measly human tried to hit my leg, but I stopped him with my speedy deflection. I squeezed his fist in mine with every ounce of my superstrength until I heard the bones in his fingers crack. He let out a high-pitched cry that was truly ugly.

These fucking humans. They chose to spend their precious time on earth hunting others. They could go anywhere. They could stand in the sun, yet time and time again, they chose darkness. I hated them with the fury of a thousand suns I could never come into contact with.

"I could kill you. I could turn you into one of us. But the truth is, you're not worthy of being a vampire. We are all-seeing and all-knowing, Jacob Sanger."

Horror struck the human's face. He was seconds away

from soiling himself.

"I'll be watching you. If I hear that any of you and your pointless organization have returned to Iceland or anywhere else on earth to hunt vampires, then there will be consequences." I dragged my fang along his neck. "Are we clear?"

Jacob nodded over and over, absolutely terrified. Did I ever look as stupid as a human?

"I need to hear you say it."

"W-we won't come to Iceland anymore, and we w-won't hunt vampires."

"Good. And remember Jacob Sanger, I'll know if you're lying."

I threw him to the ground, and little Jacob scurried away faster than a frightened cat. I grabbed his two fellow slayers and threw them down the path. They knocked into Jacob, and all three tumbled down like bowling pins. They quickly got up and continued running like the dickens.

I stared them down until they were out of sight, the rage cauldron inside me continuing to simmer. Kilroy coughed on the ground, snapping me out of my glare.

"Kilroy!"

I untied him and felt his arms and legs for any injuries. Before he could say anything, I pulled him into a warm, deep hug. His salty smell gave me comfort.

"You're safe," I whispered over and over to him.

He stared at me with his warm, wounded eyes. "Magnus, I'm okay. I'm sorry I didn't listen to you."

"It's okay." I rubbed his back. I needed to keep doing things so I didn't have to stop and think about what happened, about what could've happened.

"I'm sorry I said those things. I didn't want to believe you."

"I understand. Your whole life changed. Things I'm used

to are new to you. I should've been more sensitive."

"You were right." Kilroy let out a sigh. "My human life is over. Period. End of sentence."

"But a new life awaits."

He looked at me surprised. "Did you just say something optimistic?"

I cracked a smile.

"Will my friends hate me now?"

"They were likely in such shock that they didn't realize it was you. They'll only remember the fun human Kilroy."

"It's a shame they can't hang with the fun vampire Kilroy." Kilroy sighed again, but he was getting it. Afterlife wasn't fair.

"I'm sorry you had a tough night," I said. "I know my vampire facts don't help. I've been described as a wet blanket on more than one occasion."

"You are totally not. Magnus, you saved my life. You were a badass. You should have your own action franchise. *I'll be watching you.* It gave me chills. How did you know his name was Jacob Sanger? Is that another special vampire superpower?"

"No. It was written on the label of his jacket. I saw it when I exposed his neck."

"Oh." Kilroy deflated a little. A magician should never reveal his tricks. "Magnus?"

"Yes?"

"Can I ask you a question?"

"Of course."

"Can I kiss you?"

Our lips came together in perfect harmony.

"Put your arms around my shoulder. I can bring us back to the hotel," I said.

"I got it." Kilroy stood up on his own. He hobbled in the

snow.

"How did you know I was here?" he asked.

"I could hear you were in trouble."

"I wasn't screaming."

"You don't need to be saying anything for me to hear you. Our enhanced hearing can tune in those we care about."

"Like finding a frequency on the radio?"

"Precisely."

"So...that means you care about me?"

"Of course I do."

"Just making sure." He nuzzled against my arm. "And for the record, I care about you, too."

Even though it'd only been a few days, we had a connection. I knew it. He knew it. Vampire feelings were intense. We knew what we wanted, and nobody wanted to waste time playing games for eternity.

Kilroy continued to limp in the snow. He wasn't strong enough to turn into a bat yet.

"Kilroy, can we drop this charade and let me carry you back?"

"Fine. But for the record, I could've made it back walking on my own."

"What is this record you keep speaking of? Our conversation isn't being transcribed."

"Was that sarcasm?"

"It was."

Kilroy rolled his eyes.

"You need to recuperate. Let's get you into bed," I said.

"Vampires don't sleep in beds. We sleep in coffins." Kilroy crossed his arms defiantly. "I have a lot to teach you."

I swept him up in my arms and launched us back to the hotel.

30

MAGNUS

Kilroy felt much better by the time we made it back to the hotel. Vampires healed quickly, and Einar brought an ice pack to help. However, the giddy smile when he saw us together was not helping.

"Groak is not a word," Kilroy said to Alvin over a game of Scrabble in the main lodge.

"Yes it is!" Alvin protested.

"It's not in the dictionary." Kilroy passed over the thick, dusty paperback, open to the G section.

"Well, of course it's not going to be in *that* dictionary. This 800-year-old vampire I hooked up with once used it all the time. Groak was at one time a legitimate English word. That's more than I can say for your word."

Alvin pointed to Kilroy's last play: BLOG.

Thus the problem of playing Scrabble with vampires who'd been around for centuries: nobody could agree on which version of English to use.

"Alvin, we agreed not to include words that hadn't been used since the eighteenth century. That was the agreement," Kilroy said.

"Groak will have more staying power than your word." Alvin flipped his hoodie over his head as if he were a moody teenager.

"Blog is a word!" Kilroy said, looking around the table to make sure he wasn't crazy. "Blogging is a thing."

"It used to be," Alvin sassed back.

Kilroy and Alvin stared each down in a stalemate that quickly turned into a laugh session.

"Al, you are a petty son of a bitch, and I am living for it." Kilroy threw his head back and chuckled.

"So when do you check out?" Alvin asked us.

"Tomorrow," I said. I stood behind Kilroy and massaged his shoulders.

"Us, too. This place pretty much clears out." Alvin played the word LOUD. It was a double word score, but with low points. We all had to take victories where we could find them. Kilroy excused himself to grab a drink from the bar, pausing the game.

Alvin reorganized his rack of letters for the fiftieth time approximately. "What do you have planned for the summer? Simon found a resort in Alaska. They have a special screen that blocks out the sun."

"I think I heard of that place." It was new. A leading architect had been bitten while at a conference in Paris a decade ago, and he had been focusing his efforts since then to make better vampire accommodations. "You'll have to let us know how it is. Where is Simon?"

"He got really high, then binged on bloodburgers thanks to the munchies, and is now sleeping it off. Vampire potheads can be just as annoying as the human ones." Alvin rolled his eyes. "You guys should come with. To Alaska."

It took me a moment to let his statement sink in. "Oh."

"You're a cool guy, Magnus. Simon and I saw you and

Gunnar at this hotel every year, but you usually kept to yourself."

I was used to being the strong, silent type. I told myself I was above needing friends, but maybe I was just afraid of social rejection.

"I was really sorry to hear about Gunnar," Alvin said. "I had someone close to me get slayed at a Joni Mitchell concert. Peace and love, my ass."

"Seriously." We traded a knowing look built on this very particular kind of grief.

"He just wanted to hear 'Both Sides Now.' He wasn't hurting anyone." Alvin shook off the sorrow. "Anyway, you and Kilroy should book a trip. We'd love to see you there."

"Yeah, we'd like that."

"We'd like what?" Kilroy asked as he slipped back into his seat with a beer.

"There's a vampire hotel in Alaska," I told him as I stroked my hand up his arm.

"Sweet! I never thought I'd want to go to Alaska, but I'm game. Next summer it is."

Next summer together. What a thought.

Kilroy looked at the clock. "You guys, you guys. I know you're not into the whole new year's thing, but we have less than a minute to go."

Alvin and I traded a look. Oh, these younguns. But I couldn't help but get excited by Kilroy's energy.

"I know it's just another year, but a lot can happen in a year," he said. "Or a week."

He squeezed my knee under the table.

"Did you want to do a real countdown?" he asked.

"I'd rather skip to sex," I whispered in his ear. A little directness never hurt anyone.

Kilroy bit his bottom lip.

"You're right. New Years is such a human thing." He pushed his Scrabble tiles onto the board. "I forfeit Alvin. I'm tired. I think I'm going to turn in for the night."

"I'm able to hear you. Super hearing, remember?" Alvin said.

"Sorry," I said back.

"Don't make too much of a mess." Alvin smiled as he cleaned off the board.

Kilroy and I stood up and headed to the stairs. We held hands as we ascended the staircase, the glimmering, dark lights of the lobby below us. It was quite a view. This place was quite magical, even more so with Kilroy here.

The giant grandfather clock chimed midnight in the corner, clanging through the cavernous room. Nobody in the lobby had any change of personality. It was another hour passing on another day, another brick in our forever. But I didn't have the same apathy toward a new year.

Kilroy pushed me against the banister and snaked his tongue into my mouth in a salty, hungry kiss. Someone was still in the celebratory spirit.

"Happy New Year," I said, catching my breath.

"I think this is going to be a great year."

"How do you suppose we ring in the new year?" I growled into the sliver of space between us.

"By taking me upstairs and groaking my brains out."

31

KILROY

I expected another round of crazy, wall-shaking sex. The competitive part of me wanted to see if we could break the furniture free of their restraints. Yet when we got to the room, things turned quiet and intimate.

Magnus dotted my face with soft, caring kisses, smoothing his thumbs over my skin and my stubble and dipping down my neck. I leaned my head back against the wall, moaning as he cascaded down my body, savoring every inch of me.

We had levitated up to the ceiling and were doing this while hanging upside down, but aside from that, it was totally normal hooking up.

Magnus undressed me, unbuttoning my shirt and kissing the bruises from my human dustup. I bit my lip, holding back a hiss of pain. He would make me feel better. His lips flicked at my nipples, teasing them into tight points. My cock was rock hard and heavy in my shorts. I grinded against him, trying to relieve some tension. With a sure hand, Magnus reached between us and stroked me over my shorts.

"God," I gasped out at his touch.

He smiled against my mouth, stroking my cock. My vision went blurry with want and lust and something even more potent brewing between us.

"This has been the best week of my vampire life," I said.

"You have a relatively small sample size to compare it to, but I appreciate the compliment all the same."

"Y'know, you could've just said 'Me too.'"

Magnus had lifetime after lifetime of days to choose from, but it didn't matter. Soon, I would, too. I couldn't wait to have more experiences with him.

I undid his shirt, starting from the bottom. I wanted to be wrapped in his strong, bearish arms. I let my hands drift across the slight pouch of belly, which somehow made him feel stronger, then moved north to his strong chest. Magnus got these muscles from life, not from a gym.

Did vampires go to the gym? How did a vampire exercise if exercise was about getting the blood flowing?

Now was so not the time to ponder these issues.

"You're moving quite expeditiously," he growled into my ear.

"What does that mean?"

"It means you're quite fast at undressing me."

I pushed Magnus's pants up to the ceiling, leaving him completely naked, as he should be. His thick cock grazed my thigh. I grabbed our dicks and stroked, fire burning in his eyes. He groaned as he rutted into my hand.

"Come, my love." Magnus took my hand and floated us softly down to the floor, as if drifting on a very horny cloud. He opened the coffin lid. "I want to take you to bed."

I didn't try and correct him. Magnus holding me in his arms in that coffin hit every button inside me like a little kid in an elevator. I wanted to be enveloped by him.

He carried me into the coffin and laid us down. He pulled me close, which wasn't difficult considering the tight quarters. It would be a weird change to be in a normal-sized coffin with him and having free room. I didn't know if I wanted to get used to that.

He turned me on my side and seconds before he breached my hole with his fingers, I stopped him.

"Magnus, could we try, uh, switching positions?"

"You mean..."

"Me on top." I wanted to experience all the benefits of same-sex sex. I was dying to be inside Magnus, to watch his body writhe under my touch.

The excited grin on his face told me he was into it. He got on his back, with me hovering over him. Yep, I was very much into guy's butts now. I gave his ass a slap as well as I could in these tight quarters.

Speaking of tight, I slid a finger inside him. He let out a sound somewhere between moan and grunt. He felt so good. I loved the feeling of his rugged body under my touch.

I pressed my cock inside him, stretching him open. He reared his head back and let out an ecstatic groan that filled me with all sorts of pleasure. He was so tight and hot and I wanted him more than ever. I fucked him in a slow rhythm, trying not to blow at the first instant. Even though I was dying to.

Magnus was the strong, reserved type, but in our coffin, he was vulnerable and all mine, jutting his ass up to meet me.

"Need you," he groaned.

And I needed him. I pulled him closer against me, two bodies becoming one.

"I'm not going anywhere," I said.

I knew he'd always have that worry, that what happened

to Gunnar could happen to me. In the future, I wouldn't be stupid enough to venture into human territory. I would be safe. I never wanted him to worry about me. I never wanted him to experience that kind of loss again.

The silence was punctured only by our heavy breathing and light moaning. I hugged him against me as I thrust deeper inside his ass.

Fuck, I was already about to come. One more pump, and I was a goner. I pitied my human self for never getting to experience this kind of pleasure.

I couldn't wait to look into his gray eyes as we came.

I rubbed my face in his chest, breathing in his manly scent. I also had to keep my head down so I didn't bang it on the lid.

"These coffins are designed taller than normal configurations to accommodate vampires of all sizes," he said, sensing my discomfort.

"And for fucking." That was probably the real reason. If the coffin maker knew any vampires, they knew what was up.

A sense of wonder dazzled in Magnus's eye as I filled him up. My abs rubbed against his leaking cock, sending me closer to the edge. I knew he was close by his desperate grunting. Our intimate sex was about to ratchet up to full-on fucking.

"Fuck me," he commanded. Was there anything hotter than a demanding bottom?

I plowed into his tight hole, sweaty tips of hair falling into my eyes. I watched his face shift to unbridled desire and felt him clench around my cock as the orgasm took hold. I had reduced my grumpy vampire to putty. His eyes burned red with hunger as he released across his stomach and chest. I pounded into his hole, emptying myself in a ravenous, all-consuming release

Damn.

Vampire sex was the best. Who needed daylight when I could have that?

32

MAGNUS

When I awoke, Kilroy was gone, and I was still naked. I went to push the coffin lid, but it was already open. Fortunately, it was night and the curtains were closed.

I rubbed sleep from my eyes and followed the only source of light in the room to the desk where Kilroy pored over his notebook.

"Good evening," Kilroy said. "Oh! I finally got it right!"

"What the devil are you working on? You've been at it all week." I didn't want to make assumptions, but Kilroy didn't strike me as the kind of guy to journal. His thoughts free-flowed from his brain to his mouth.

Kilroy slapped the notebook shut before I could get a peek. Sneaking up on a vampire with enhanced senses was as fruitful as playing basketball against a very tall person.

"I didn't mean to intrude."

"It's cool. It's ready."

"It's ready?"

"Yeah. Here." Kilroy opened the notebook to the middle page and handed it over.

I cocked my head. He had drawn the face of a man who looked familiar, but I couldn't place him.

"Do you know who that is?"

I kept staring, trying to figure out where I knew this gentleman from. He had a refined look to him. Thick eyebrows, long nose, sharp jaw. His features ignited some kind of recognition in me, but I was unable to connect the dots. It was as if I'd forgotten a word that I once used regularly.

"Can you give me a hint?" I asked.

"Magnus." Kilroy tilted his head, his eyes containing a glimmer of pity in them. "That's you."

I gawked at the drawing with such an overwhelming sense of nostalgia, I slumped down to the floor.

"That's me?" Memories flooded back for me. The mornings I spent perfecting my hair in the mirror, time that I thought I was wasting in the moment, but now I treasured like the warm hug of my mother. I thought back on catching my reflection in windows, or on spoons at dinner parties, or in the pond behind my house.

My house!

"I had a house! There was a pond behind it, and when I would take walks into town, I made sure to pass it so I could see my reflection. I had a house adjacent to a pond! I remember!"

"Like from when you were a human?"

I ran my fingers over the features to see how they corresponded to Kilroy's sketch. I felt the small bump at the bridge of my nose. I brushed along my sideburns, which miraculously managed to stay even despite shaving without a mirror.

"I got this scar when I tripped over my dog. Do you know what that means? I had a dog!"

The faint image of a Golden Retriever with warm eyes popped into my head. Did I get to say goodbye to them?

"That's so cool!"

"He wasn't the most useful dog. Completely unhelpful on hunts." I had a flash of him rolling around on the grass. Was it during a hunt? A walk through the woods? I didn't know. It was such an insignificant memory, but it meant the world to me. It was quite incredible the little bits of minutia we remembered from the past.

"You are remarkably talented. The detailing is stunning."

"I used to draw," Kilroy said. "It helped me stay zen before surfs."

I pointed to the sketch and burst out laughing in unbridled joy. "That's my face!"

"You have a beautiful face."

I rested a hand on my cheek and a tear slid over my fingers. Then more tears. It poured out of me. For hundreds of years, I lived in a space of anonymity, a void without a past.

"Thank you," I said, my voice cracking.

"Magnus, I'm sorry. I didn't mean to upset you."

"You're not." I stared at the sketch, then at the beautiful man who had the heart and talent to draw it. "I love you, Kilroy."

It was soon, but what did time matter to people who lived eternally? After centuries on this planet, I knew who I was and what I wanted. Gunnar would always remain in my heart, but it was big enough for Kilroy, too. The heart had four chambers, after all.

Shock crossed his face, but only for a moment. He squatted down and kissed me.

"I love you, too."

"You don't have to say it just because I said it."

"I'm not. I'm going to be wandering this world for a good, long while. And I'd like to do it with you." He threaded our fingers together and brought them to his lips. "At first, I was kinda freaked out by the whole immortality thing. I mean, forever is a long-ass time. But I feel better knowing I won't have to do it alone."

For the first time in a long while, I was excited about the future. I was actually grateful to be a vampire. My sketch smiled back at me, letting me know everything would be okay.

EPILOGUE

SOME TIME LATER…BUT WHAT WAS TIME TO A VAMPIRE?

Magnus

Kilroy approached me at the front desk.

"Magnus, I have two questions. Question one: if vampires are unable to reproduce, then what are we ejaculating when we come?"

Of course, he had to ponder this in public, in front of our first guests waiting to check in. I didn't possess a mirror, which made me unable to see how red my face was.

"What's question number two?" I grumbled through gritted teeth.

"Where did we put the extra blood-flavored mints for the pillows?"

"Top shelf. Supply closet."

"Sweet!" He gave me a double thumbs up and left me to deal with a pair of slack-jawed guests, an older man and woman in their swimsuits.

"He's very inquisitive. How can I help you?"

"We need extra towels."

"Ah yes." I grabbed two from under my desk and handed them over.

They thanked me, then walked out the door that led to the ocean. The moonlight reflected on the whitecaps of the waves.

"It's a great night for a swim," Kilroy said, suddenly back at my side, mints stacked on the counter. His gold name tag shimmered in the light.

"It's always a great night for a swim. We're in paradise."

"How do you like it?" Kilroy leaned over the counter, showing off his toned arms. "Living in paradise?"

He ran a finger over the Hawaiian lei around my neck.

"If you'd told me two years ago that I would be a co-owner of a beach resort on Kauai, I never would have believed you."

"You didn't answer my question."

"There's a myriad of questions of yours that I shall not be answering." I leaned closer, our faces barely apart. We probably should not have been flirting openly in front of guests. Fortunately, our clientele was easygoing. The islands did that to a person, made all their regular anxieties fade away.

After our trip to Alaska, Kilroy became intent on finding more places where he could surf and enjoy the sun. Beaches weren't just for humans, he told me over and over.

We came to this hotel nestled in the Kilauea Volcano on the Hawaiian island of Kauai and fell in love. Who knew a place this lovely could produce button-down shirts so garish? Kilroy taught me to surf on the water; we made love on the beach and atop palm trees.

Likeke, the conduit hotel proprietor, wanted to retire, and we took it as a sign that this was where we were meant to be. He spent his last few months showing us the ropes, making for a seamless transition. The only thing we were missing was a conduit like Likeke or Einar. Likeke had put the word out to others in the community like him, and he promised the right person would show up in time.

We had time. We were vampires, after all.

Until then, Kilroy and I made it work. I cherished being able to put my energy and time into building a business that other vampires could enjoy. So many thanked us for keeping the hotel open; it had hosted so many wonderful memories for them. Alvin and Simon showed up every year, and we'd usually go midnight snorkeling with them.

The only time we closed the hotel was the week after Christmas. We couldn't not make our annual pilgrimage to Iceland. Einar and Reynar also provided excellent advice for running a hotel.

"We are having high tide tomorrow, and Magnus, you are getting back on the water." Kilroy came around to my side of the desk and nibbled at my ear, sending jolts of heat across my skin. This was no doubt highly unprofessional, but I waited a few seconds before stepping away. That was a perk of the job. Kilroy and I were around each other all the time, and he looked so damn cute in his outfit. It was hours-long foreplay.

"Maybe surfing isn't for me." I had tried surfing on the water and ingested so much salt water that I could've cured the sore throats of the entire human population.

"Don't say that! Just because you wiped out once or twice...or more...that doesn't mean you should quit. Get back on that surfboard."

The thrill of watching a wave crest above me was cut short by being thrown around in the water as if I were a piece of laundry in a washing machine. My core could only engage so much.

But I couldn't say no to that cute face. "Fine. I will try one more time."

"Good."

"Not because I enjoy it. I don't enjoy having my legs thrown up in the air."

"Are you sure?" he growled in my ear.

Fuck. I was proverbial putty in his very real hands. It was a good thing we bolted down all the furniture in our room.

I could only imagine the reviews on Vampire Vacations. *Nice furnishings but the co-owners couldn't stop dry humping.*

My mind was about to travel to very naughty places. But the head of every vampire in the lobby turned to a woman walking up to my desk.

A human woman.

She was petite but had a fire about her, one of those women who were tough thanks to being in a male-dominated field. Her aviator sunglasses were perched on her hand and her oversized T-shirt and ripped jeans gave me the impression that I should not be messing with her.

She ignored the looks on the vampires she passed. I didn't have the same sense of panic as I did when I usually saw humans in the flesh.

"Hello. How can I, uh, help you tonight?" I asked.

The woman opened her mouth to give her name, but Kilroy beat her to it.

"Amelia?"

Kilroy

Of all the vampire resorts in all the world, I didn't expect my human former friend to walk through those doors. The last time we saw each other, she and my other former friends were screaming and trying to get away from me.

"Hi, Kilroy."

"What brings you here? How did you even get in here?" Amelia seemed different. True, it'd been a while since we last saw each other, but you could tell with good friends. She had the look of a person who'd been through shit.

I turned to Magnus, who seemed remarkably calm considering a human was in our midst.

"I saw you in Iceland. You were the vampire who came to the party at the Black Fortress."

I nodded yes. I remembered the flick of recognition on her face before she raced out of that room and left me with vampire hunters.

"You were the first vampire I'd ever seen up close, and it triggered something in me. It made me want to learn more about them. I wasn't scared like Biff was."

"You have the gene," Magnus said.

Amelia took out a DNA test and held it up. "I was adopted when I was a baby. I tracked down my birth parents. It turns out that I am part of a lineage of humans who can co-exist with vampires. Our people have worked with vampires for millennia, keeping them in the shadows but still connected to the human world.

"I've been training, learning how to harness my powers. And then I wanted to find you, Kilroy."

My heart lit up, and I had trouble keeping a stoic look on my face. "You did?"

"I searched the world and finally found you here. I wanted to apologize for that night."

I bowed my head. It was traumatic, and I wasn't fully over it, but I was happy to have her here.

"It's okay. I get it. Vampires are scary. It's a good thing we don't have mirrors or else I'd probably scare myself."

"I wanted to see you because...I miss my friend."

"I missed you, too." I mourned my human life; the memories were starting to fade little by little.

"How would you like to work here?" Magnus asked her. "We're looking for a human who could work with us, be our conduit."

"Vampires are much chiller than humans. Plus you get days to yourself, obviously," I said.

"I'd love to."

I stepped around the desk and hugged her. I had a friend back.

"And this is Magnus." We held hands so she could see we were a couple. "Oh by the way, I'm bisexual now. It's a vampire thing."

No time like the present to come out.

Magnus led her to get started. I smiled out at the lobby, at Amelia, at Magnus, and this wonderful life we'd created. How lucky was I? Fuck sunlight. Being a vampire was the absolute best.

"I'm giving this one more try, then I'm done," Magnus said.

We were in the ocean on another gorgeous, warm night, the sky sprinkled with a vibrant display of stars. Magnus and I sat on our surfboards. I was my usual relaxed self, while he was at the end of his rope.

"We've been at this for months. I know you can do it." I appreciated that Magnus was trying to learn how to surf. It was my thing, and as much as I wanted it to be his thing, too,

I would be cool if it ultimately wasn't. But surfing was the closest I ever got to touching God, and I wanted to share that feeling with the man I loved.

Magnus had gotten me into reading more, which was a Magnus thing that was becoming my thing. I was learning all the stuff I could've studied in college. Last week, I read a book about microbiology—and I liked it!

After months of wipeouts, I promised Magnus this would be the last time we tried. The man had put in a valiant effort. In fairness, the tides were stronger at night. It was awesome for experienced surfers like me, but more of a challenge for newbies.

"Okay, here comes another one. This one looks epic!" I signaled for him to hop up onto his surfboard. Magnus wore a Hawaiian-style bathing suit with pretty pink flowers. All this attempted surfing had also given him a more defined chest. There was still a little paunch in the midsection, but it was covering a solid wall of abdominals. In short, my vampire boyfriend had only gotten more fuckable since we'd been together.

I paddled closer to the wave, Magnus following my lead.

"Remember to engage your core!"

"I'm aware!"

"Keep your knees slightly bent. Find your balance point." I yelled to him. He was at my side. Could we do this tandem?

The dark water pulled up in front of us, a wall of saltwater ready to be conquered. As it curled over, I pushed into the tailpipe.

"C'mon!" I prayed to every God I could think of that Magnus would make it through.

"I think…I'm actually doing it," he said.

And he was! He was shaky but balancing, a model surfer

on display. His face was stamped with abject fear, but he was still doing it.

"Yes! That's it!"

We moved up and surfed along the top of the wave, as if it were a volcano. I looked out on the beach and shore, feeling tall and mighty.

"This is amazing!" Magnus loosened up, and his face went alive with wonder. After centuries on this planet, he could still find the beauty in something new. He was viewing nature from a brand-new angle and pushing his limits. That was what living was all about, even for those of us who were dead.

The wave receded, sending us back into the water. We swam to shore. I sat on the beach and watched Magnus come in with the waves. I drank blood from a canteen.

"We should go back out there," Magnus said when he emerged from the water looking like a freaking swimsuit model. He smiled wide, his fangs catching a glint of moonlight.

"Drink up." I handed over the canteen. He gulped it down. "How does it feel?"

"Incredible. I was…I was levitating on water. I know I could always levitate if I wanted to, but it's different to do it on an unruly wave."

"It's pretty wicked."

"It's extremely wicked." He dropped the canteen in the sand, then looked at me with a hungry gaze. The thrill of victory had sparked a fire in his eyes.

He pushed me into the sand, climbed on top, and devoured me in a kiss. His salty lips and rough hands explored my body, setting me aflame. A wave crashed over us, but it couldn't stop us from making out.

"Ready to go again?" he asked.

"Are you talking about sex or surfing?"

He laughed against my lips.

He pulled me to my feet. We grabbed our surfboards and ran back into the water.

This was the ~~life~~ afterlife.

Thanks for reading!

Only One Coffin was my first toe-dip into the paranormal genre. I hope you liked it!

Please consider leaving a review on the book's Amazon page or on Goodreads. Reviews are crucial in helping other readers find new books.

To get access to free stories, plus sneak peeks on my new books, join my newsletter.

If you enjoy age gaps and forced proximity, check out my free contemporary novella *Three Nights with the Manny*, available exclusively for newsletter subscribers.

Join the party in my Facebook Group. Follow me at Bookbub to be alerted to new releases.

And then there's email. I love hearing from readers! Send me a note anytime at info@ajtruman.com. I always respond.

ALSO BY A.J. TRUMAN

South Rock High
Ancient History

Drama!

Romance Languages

Single Dads Club
The Falcon and the Foe

The Mayor and the Mystery Man

The Barkeep and the Bro

Browerton University Series
Out in the Open

Out on a Limb

Out of My Mind

Out for the Night

Out of This World

Outside Looking In

Out of Bounds

Seasonal Novellas
Fall for You

You Got Scrooged

Hot Mall Santa

ABOUT THE AUTHOR

A.J. Truman is a gay man who writes books with **humor, heart, and hot guys.** What else does a story need? He lives in a very full house in Indiana with his husband, son, and pets. He loves happily ever afters and sneaking off for an afternoon movie.

www.ajtruman.com
info@ajtruman.com
The Outsiders - Facebook Group

Printed in Great Britain
by Amazon